Seven Days

COFFEE JONES

Contents

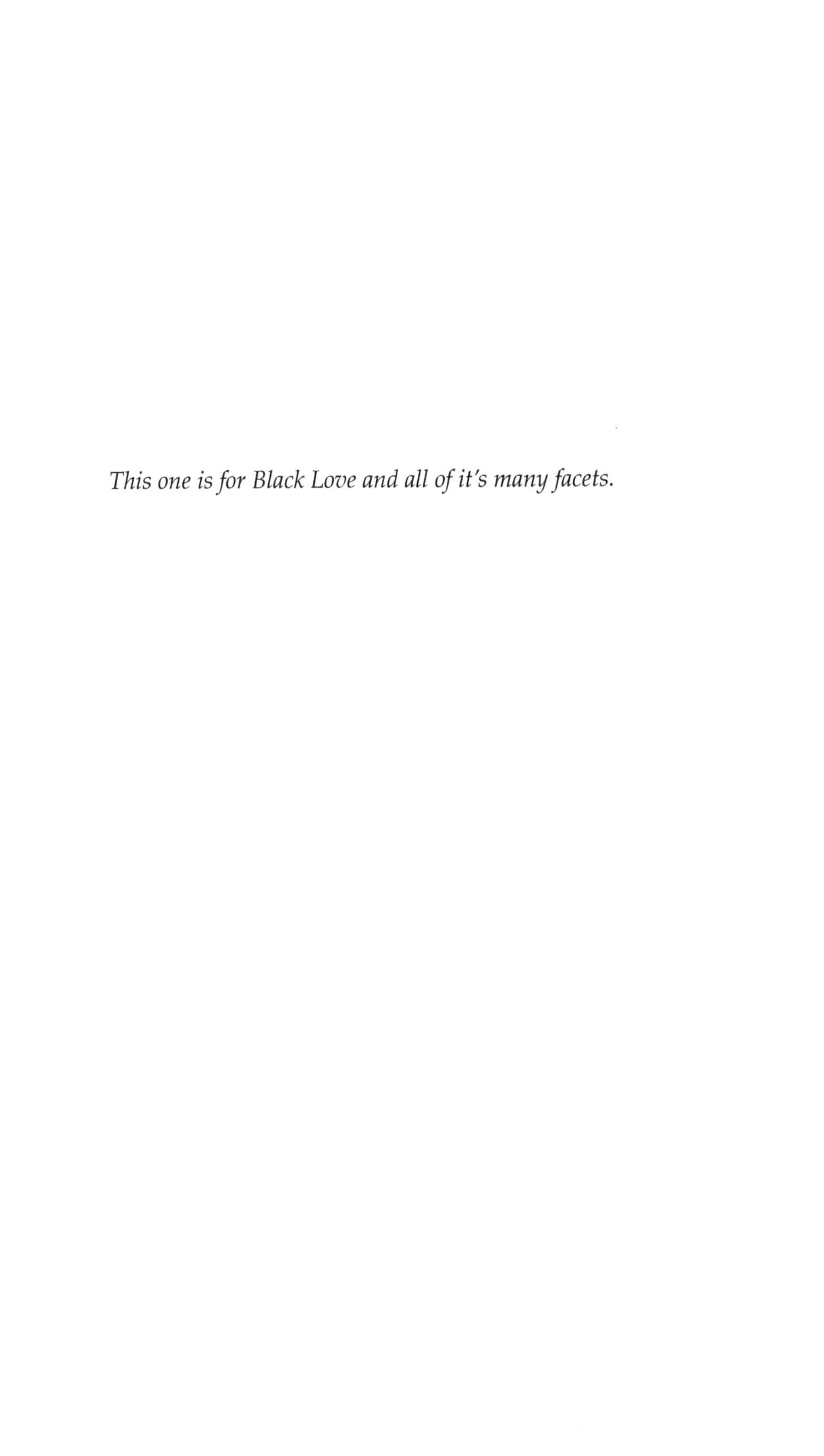

This one is for Black Love and all of it's many facets.

KWANZAA GUIDE

KWANZAA IS A YEARLY HOLIDAY WHICH TAKES PLACE BETWEEN DECEMBER 26TH AND JANUARY 1ST. IT CELEBRATES BLACK CULTURE AND WAS CREATED BY A BLACK ACTIVIST NAMED MAULANA KARENGA. THE FIRST KWANZAA TOOK PLACE IN 1966. EACH DAY, WE OBSERVE ONE PRINCIPLE FROM NGUZO SABA (N-GU-ZO SAH-BAH) OR THE SEVEN PRINCIPLES OF KWANZAA.

DAY 1 — **UMOJA (UNITY)**
To strive for and maintain unity in the family, community, nation, and race.

DAY 2 — **KUJICHAGULIA (SELF-DETERMINATION)**
To define ourselves, name ourselves, create for ourselves, and speak for ourselves.

DAY 3 — **UJIMA (COLLECTIVE WORK & RESPONSIBILITY)**
To build and maintain our community together and make our brother's and sister's problems our problems and to solve them together.

DAY 4 — **UJAMAA (COOPERATIVE ECONOMICS)**
To build and maintain our own stores, shops, and other businesses and to profit from them together.

DAY 5 — **NIA (PURPOSE)**
To make our collective vocation the building and developing of our community in order to restore our people to their traditional greatness.

DAY 6 — **KUUMBA (CREATIVITY)**
To do always as much as we can, in the way we can, in order to leave our community more beautiful and beneficial than we inherited it.

DAY 7 — **IMANI (FAITH)**
To believe with all our heart in our people, our parents, our teachers, our leaders, and the righteousness and victory of our struggle.

Pronunciation Guide

Xaevi = Zavee

Olaya = Olayuh

Zaraki = Za-ra-kee

Niwibwe = Ni-wib-way

Novali = No-va-lee

Chyna = China

Ezri = Ezree

Kenji = Ken-jee

Kocoum = Ko-coo-um

Isra = Is-ruh

Bratan = Brah-tan

Umoja = oo-MO-jah

Kujichagulia = koo-jee-chah-GOO-lee-ah

Ujima = oo-JEE-mah

Ujamaa = oo-jah-MAH-ah

Nia = NEE-ah

Kuumba = koo-OOM-bah

Imani = ee-MAH-nee

 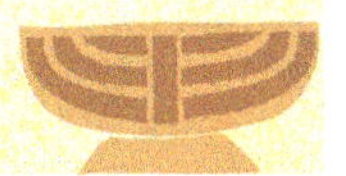

One

Psalm Rose

"SHIT," I mutter.

My suitcase slips from my hands and nearly trips me. The LA air is the only thing that makes me unfocused.

Thankfully, my driver meets me halfway and saves me from the rest of my suitcases. Kwanzaa season is upon us, and it is gearing up to be a celebration. We have seven days to highlight, support, and uplift the Black community through partying, eating, and philanthropy. It's usually the best time of year, but never without a little bit of drama.

We get into the car quickly and the tires hug the familiar road home, and soon, I am standing in front of the imposing front door. My mother is waiting for me. I swallow hard, my face remembering her favorite smile, and I slide it into place.

"Psalm, welcome home!" she squeals, yanking me into her arms.

"You cut it extremely close. You should have been home weeks ago."

"There were a few sample evaluations we had to finish. We're testing a new soil composition for the fields in LA."

Her slender hand waves my words away. "Yes, yes. You still should have made it home. You've missed all the pre-Kwanzaa events."

Thank Yah.

"Not to mention, your tattoo ceremony is in two days."

"We will be ready," I mutter.

"Psalm! This is a big deal. It officially welcomes you into womanhood. You will be marked as one of Yah's eternal daughters. Every woman in this Nation, going back to the founders, has gotten this tattoo."

"I know, Mama! That's why we picked out the dress months ago, scheduled my makeup, bought the shoes, and picked the venue. I am completely ready."

Her knife pauses in the bell pepper that she is slicing.

"Honey, it's not just about those things. Every woman in our family will be there to see you become a woman."

"Why? This is supposed to be for the immediate family only," I whine.

"Oh, hush, girl. We are hosting Kwanzaa this year anyway, so it was natural for me to invite them. They have been asking about you. Since you spend nearly all your time in Bali, we hardly see you."

"I'm working. You know, keeping the family business going?"

"That's not supposed to be your job. You have parents and brothers for that."

"I love my work."

"Unfortunately for all of us," Mom snaps.

The kitchen goes quiet before a symphony of feet interrupts us. Everyone heard me arrive and came to greet me.

"Psalm is home," Chanson, my youngest brother, announces.

"We were starting to think you weren't going to come home this year," my youngest sister Chyna adds.

"I would never miss Kwanzaa. It's *the* holiday season after all."

Despite my mom trying to sour things for me, I love the holidays. Growing up, it was the most magical time of the year, and I am determined for it to be just that. As we got older, me and my siblings made a pact to always make it back for Kwanzaa, no matter what. So there is no way I wasn't going to make it back home.

"Where's Novali?"

"She'll be here in time for your ceremony. They had last-minute business in Paris."

"Alright, let's get lunch ready," Mom says, assigning us all to stations.

The air had returned to the room. Instantly relaxing me. I will let it go for now and bask in their love. My siblings made everything better.

Soul

The driveway is nearly overflowing when my car pulls in.

My head plops down on the steering wheel. I can do this. It's just one week out of the entire year. *This is no big deal, and I am blessed to have such a big family.* If I keep telling myself those things, I can make it through the week.

I had walked right into a pre-Kwanzaa garden party

My loafers hit the stone path, garnering the attention of the few people near the door. A smile carries me through the crowd. Unfortunately, my mom's church friends snatch me up.

"Soul! We haven't seen you in such a long time. Where have you been?"

"In New York, I just finished my third solo exhibition. The city is nice but, It's great to be home."

"I know your father will be happy you're back."

"Speaking of which, let me go find him. Excuse me."

That conversation had to be cut short. It is no secret that my dad has been itching to retire. He can't do that without his successor. It's my birthright to run the family business. My father has built the largest tech company in the Nation's history. I grew up inside this company. Tech became a passion from the very beginning. My early work displayed signs of the genius to come. It was proof that no one would have to worry when it was my turn to take over. The position has been held by the eldest male child in the family since the beginning of the Nation. There is weight and prestige attached to generational positions, an honor to anyone offered the opportunity. Still, it doesn't feel like an honor to me. It feels like a restriction, like a barrier to something better, and I don't have the heart to tell my dad that, so I avoid him.

Instead, I go to my room, and getting there is no easy feat. Dodging house guests is a specialty of mine, considering I am the oldest. But my brother isn't far behind. He had returned home from USC weeks ago and was waiting for me to show up.

"Well, well, well. If it isn't Mr. Basquiat," Tade jokes, leaning against the door frame.

"What's up, pledge?"

He examines my bookshelf.

"Nothing much. Seeing your calm, Dad can't know you're here yet." He chuckles.

"Please, tell me he is going to be chill this year?"

"Not on your life."

I flop on the bed, taking in the patterned ceiling.

"Kwanzaa hasn't been enjoyable in a while, and I want it to be this time."

"Maybe if you don't spend most of the year in New York, it could be."

He pauses, unsure.

"It feels like you're running."

I am.

Running is the only way for me to make peace with my path. Eventually, New York will be a thing of the past, and so will my career in the arts. With the time I have left, I hope to put myself on the world map instead of just the Nation's map. My dad's legacy is tied to this place, and I don't want mine to be. It would kill me to tell Dad that. His legacy is all he wants to discuss whenever I'm in town. Tade isn't aware of that so he isn't looking out for Dad when he drags me back to the party.

"Someone else wants to see you." Tade tosses over his shoulder.

Isra is sitting on the couch with a glass of wine in hand.

Fashionable as always. She is working the crowd, and I watch in awe and fear because when she is done with them, she will start with me.

"I was beginning to think I only had two brothers, but here you are."

"Isra, where's your business?"

"Right in front of me," she scowls, crossing her arms over her chest. She drags me out onto the patio, her eyes trained on the flowers blooming in the garden. "Why is this my first time seeing you in months?"

Isra's anger is replaced with sadness. Being the two oldest, we have bonded the most. It's hard being away from her. She has her husband and her daughter to keep her company, but there is nothing like sibling love. Plus, I haven't been here for many of those milestones either.

"I'm sorry. Truly. My third solo show just wrapped, and it took us an entire year to prepare for that. Creating consumes me sometimes."

"I know," Isra mutters, leaving so much unsaid.

"Anyway, let's make a pact to enjoy the holidays."

"Deal."

The day passes without incident, and it's time to link up. In addition to missing my family, I missed my friends. We have been tight since diapers, most of us coming from essential families. Some families in the Nation have essential privileges that allow us to travel more than others. We also can live outside of Nation territories.

Juke sets up pool games in the basement, so we agree to meet there. Music thumps through the speakers as we arrive. Juke is already drunk and somehow snuck some base into holiday music. My spirit picks up. By the time we make it down the stairs, we are dancing.

Juke starts a game with me, and Diana sparks up.

"Come on. Come on. What has everybody been up to?" Diana asks around a cloud of smoke.

"Bump that we need to talk about these rumors on Jiacom," Kenji interjects.

"What rumors?" Xaevi asks.

"War rumors. My boy, who is in the crew, told me they've been talking about going to war with the Dominicans. Certain men have been getting drafted through anonymous letters."

"No way, the Nation has never been to war before. Something is always worked out," Tree adds.

"Anything is possible," I chime in.

"Guys, this is a time of celebration. If there is a war coming, we can't do anything about it. Let's focus on the now."

Diana forces a shot of whisky into my hand, and we relent.

A couple more shots, and we are doing Karaoke. Tree is singing Jodeci off-key while Diana is capturing it all on camera. It warms my heart to see the band back together. We are all off doing things. Diana is on track to be the first woman heart surgeon in the Nation's history. She is also getting married next year. Kenji is a literary genius with multiple best-selling books. Tree is a once-in-a-lifetime soccer star. Juke is a celebrated pianist, and Xaevi is an Olympic track prodigy. We are on the move. Consequently, there is less time for each other. It had been months since we had hung out individually and at least a year since we were all in the same room.

It makes me sad that we have so little time for each other

while we are in the best parts of life. We are growing older, and the reality of it all is setting in on me. It unceasingly does in LA. The longer I am here, the harder it is to keep a smile on my face. Juke tosses me a bottle of water, bringing me back to the present. We have today, and for now, that's enough.

Psalm

Isolation is the best part of tattoo day.

This time is supposed to be for reflection. The goal is to meditate on my womanhood, everything that led me to this point, and on my relationship with Yah. There is nothing more important to me than him. Yah is my comfort in every battle I go in with my mother and with every obstacle I face in my life. He is essential to my journey, and this tattoo binds me to him and all the women past, present, and future in the Nation. It aligns us under one heartbeat. The fact that my mom thinks I take this honor lightly is more proof of our distance. It makes me more grateful for the lavender and cinnamon-scented water around me and even more grateful that Novali was here to guide me into womanhood, so Mom and I don't have to fight through it together.

Normally, a woman is married when they get their tattoo. It is almost taboo that I am not. I think about that, too. Everything floods my mind, and it makes my heart ache for home. The view from Woz River Valley calls to me. Mom regularly says Bali never felt like home to her. It doesn't feel like home to anyone, even though we spent all my life there. We barely lived in Los Angeles, yet Mom expects me to want to be here. Apprenticing with my grandmother pushed me deeper into the forests and biomes of Indonesia. In every way, my heart is tied to nature, to her growth and prosperity. Mom would find me in the trees or picking through the mud. She despised my lack of interest in "womanly" things. Mom thinks it is why I never took an interest in romantic relationships. They feel like a distraction to me. There will be a time for that, but right now, I want to become the Vice President of Botanical Security, which will take some dedication. But I feel close. My research is going to be the icing on the cake that is my application.

A soft knock on the door brings me out of my reverie.

Novali enters the room in her niqab and dumps a wooden bucket of warm basil water over my head. She prays over me, then rubs me down. Her henna-patterned hands cover me in hibiscus paste, finishing my fingertips with turmeric paste. Finally, she braids a henna mixture into my hair, covering it with a white veil. I pray while she gathers my dress. It's a full-skirt dress cinched at the waist, decorated in silk-sown flora and fauna. Novali slips white flats on my perfumed feet and leads me to the garden where the women are waiting.

There is not one man in sight as Novali fastens the white veil before leading me down the aisle. Every woman stands looking up at the sky. Until I am tattooed, they aren't allowed to look at me. At this moment, I am an offering to Yah. The only one who can lay eyes on me is the tattoo artist. Only the queen knows her name. She is wearing a niqab as well. Novali places me in the chair, and the women bow, face to the floor while I am marked for Yah. Tattoos aren't ideal for me, but I will do anything for my faith. She parts the translucent bell sleeves and starts the hour-long process. People tell never-ending tattoo horror stories, but this isn't bad. It's like being pinched forever. It is also pleasant to see my mom humbled, even if it is for just an hour.

Once the tattoo artist is done, I am patched up. Novali bows with me before the crowd and takes me to the back to wash my hair and style it. My veil covers my face completely as we leave the gardens and go back home. I am starting to struggle with the silence, but thankfully, we arrive home quickly. Novali guides me into the house, where she removes both of our veils, revealing to me the packed dining room.

"Surprise!" they all shout.

I was taken aback. Novali squeezes my hand to remind me to keep it off my face, so I share their excitement for as long as possible. As soon as my mom has a free moment, we have a conversation.

"A party?"

"Psalm, you are worth celebrating. My goal was to celebrate you. How am I wrong this time?"

"It just would have been nice to come home to a smaller party is all."

"This is Kwanzaa season. No party is going to be small."

"It feels like you're up to something," I snap.

So, what if I am?" she replies.

"Knock it off, please."

"Psalm, you have been floating around Bali with your head in the clouds while the rest of us make sacrifices. It is time for you to do your part in this family. This is the last I am going to speak about it tonight."

A quiet sound starts echoing in my ears, and I realize it's my breathing. *Fuck, this could not happen right now.* I scurry out of the kitchen. Every inch of the sprawling property feels like it's covered with people who want to talk, offer their congratulations, ask about the family, and whatever else stops me from being alone.

I go up to my room, stroll out to the balcony, and drop my secret ladder. Dad and I had put together a room on the roof that no one else knew about. It's hidden behind the tall walls and overflowing greenery all over the property. Mom repeatedly says our home should look like we are botanists. The room is small. Most of the space is outside, so I can sleep under the stars.

The pressure in my chest lightens, and I light up the stash of joints that I keep hidden away. Watching the smoke curl up to greet the stars makes my shoulders drop and a sigh slip from my lips. The worst of it is over. The spotlight is off of me and back on the holidays. My mom's friends and cousins would have better things to focus on than me.

Soul

The sunlight reminds me we shouldn't have had so many shots last night. When I stumble into the kitchen, my mom is talking a mile a minute.

"We have the Unity Party, food drives, community clean-ups, Kwanzaa village, Fundraiser night..."

"Mother, please," I groan as Isra puts a steaming cup in front of me.

"And all of you better update your social calendars so we know what other Kwanzaa activities you are participating in."

"Mom!" Tade exclaims.

"Vera, please give the children a break and check on breakfast," Dad interjects, sitting next to me at the dining room table.

His presence is enough to shift the energy in the room. My dad used to be my best friend. We are the closest out of everybody. He is the person who introduced me to the arts. We spent hours and hours wasting time on his fishing boat, sometimes coming home with nothing. It makes this rift between us more painful.

"Soul, it's wonderful to have you home," he offers.

"It's good to be back, Dad. I missed you."

"I missed you too, son."

The serving staff lay the table out with the complete breakfast. We all indulge, relaxing into our loud family dynamic. This is what made me ache for home when things get hectic in New York. Sure, I have reached my current peak. Soul Niwibwe is one of the most celebrated up-and-coming artists. My sculptures and oil paintings have hit the mainstream, and people are spending big money to see my artwork every day. It's awe-inspiring and addicting. There is no way my dad would get me to let go of this feeling right now. There is plenty of youth left in me and much more to accomplish.

After breakfast Isra, Tade, and I go around helping people put up their decorations, clean up their lawns, and carry in their groceries. It is our favorite holiday tradition. We get to help the community, get Mom off our backs, and get some time to ourselves. Today, we are helping Mrs. Johnson move her furniture out of her storage room. Tade is in rare form, which means he is very annoying.

"I'm just saying it would be way cooler if you moved back here."

"And it would be even cooler if you moved with me."

"Watch it, Soul," Isra says, pointing at me.

"Tade lay off. He gets it enough from Mom as is, and I have something way more important to talk about." She smirks.

"So, Soul, why are you still single?"

"Because pagan pussy is hard to stay out of," I whisper.

Tade burst out in laughter, gaining a look from Mrs. Johnson. Isra is nearly red in the face. Her fist is balled up so tight I skip ahead.

"Soul, say some more stupid shit and see what happens," she threatens.

"Was I supposed to lie? Pagan women are easy. Once they see my name and accolades, the panties come off."

"Do you kiss your mother with that mouth?"

"Only on the cheek."

"You're a lost cause," Isra says, throwing up her hands.

Mr. Johnson calls us to finish moving the furniture. Once we get everything set in stone, they send us away with small bags filled with Kwanzaa treats. I push the money aside and pop a warm sweet potato mini muffin into my mouth. My shoulders instantly slump. This is what we love most about home. There is so much love here, especially during Kwanzaa. It's almost like being a kid again. There is safety within the community. Life has snatched that from me. Growing up has taken me away from my home, or maybe it was just fear of the future itself.

Tade turned stoic for once. "Seriously, Soul, what's the holdup?"

He pulls me closer as we walk home. "Dad has been introducing me to families. He's talking about marriages. It would be nice to have some guidance."

"Dad and other men in the fam—"

"But they aren't in our immediate family, and they aren't my big brother."

"He has a point," Isra sings.

"My schedule doesn't allow me to date seriously right now. In time, it will, but planning for my fourth show has already started."

"We know your art is important to you, but maybe there is a woman out there who will help you plan your shows ... and run the family business," Isra adds.

Another conversation that can spoil the day.

"Let's focus on the holidays. Isra, don't you have abayas that are ready to be picked up?"

"Why, yes. This way, fellas."

Psalm

Novali's arm in mine makes me feel giddy. The only bad part about being in Bali is being without her. Mom typically leaves me alone when we are together. Novali is the perfect example for me. She got married to Kocoum when she was twenty years old, and they have twin boys. Novali gave up her lawyer dreams to raise her children. She is supposed to be my aspiration. Mom wants me to follow in my sister's footsteps. I had delayed it long enough. She wants me to get married and have children, seeing I graduate college early. It is the eventual option for me. My duty would be done, and my mother would be off my back, but I don't want to give up my dreams the way Novali has.

Today, mom set us free on the town. There are a lot of people out, shopping, grabbing meals, visiting each other's houses. You truly get a chance to see everyone who lives in our community. Novali and I grab street food as we walk. Even though the Nation is spread out across states and countries, every section felt like home. Well, except LA. We have been to the faction in Paris, Morocco, and lived in Bali. They all feel cozy, but LA feels like a different ball game. People care who you are here. If you have some status, they post your business across Jiacom, our private social media site. Our family has been repeat victims of the scrutiny.

"Psalm, are you paying attention?" Novali interrupts.

"You said Mom designed these abayas, so they aren't going to be my style," I answer while tossing my clam shell.

"Ha! You know mom doesn't care about that. She just wants you pretty and posing. Plus, the traditional style suits you."

"Oh no, is this when you tell me what mom's plan is?"

"You know she isn't giving that up," she laments.

Our seamstress got me into mom's first look, and traditional is an understatement. The fabric climbs up my neck to a nearly uncomfortable height.

"She just wants to ensure we are all presentable because everyone will be in town."

"This is beyond presentable."

"There are a few looks from Paris in your wardrobe for the week. Mom wouldn't let me do too much."

"You are a lifesaver."

Once everything is sent back to the house, we go out for tea.

"So, how are the boys?"

"Amazing. We are going to try to visit more. I can't wait for you to see them, Psalm. They are talking and walking now."

"It's a shame they don't get to visit often."

Her excitement nearly turns to sadness before she puts that signature smile back on her face.

"Kocoum got promoted again and likes to keep his family nearby. I enjoy being there for him."

"So marriage is good?"

"It's great. I get to shop, eat, and style my heart away. The boys are loved and taken care of. We live in a beautiful house in a beautiful country."

"Propaganda. Propaganda. Tell me how you truly feel."

Novali adjusts her already perfect head wrap. If my hunch is correct, my mom will put me on the marriage market this year, and knowing what to expect from a marriage is an important insight for me to have.

"It's work. Marriage isn't going to be easy, but it's worth it. I am independent and well-loved."

"You said he snores," I interject.

"And the snoring doesn't bother me much. It's worth it. Pinky promise."

She laughs and pushes me to change the subject. Novali isn't telling me the whole truth. She doesn't want to discourage me. It's in her eyes and the way she holds her shoulders. Something is either up in her marriage or with the institution in general. But she isn't going to share that with me. Mom would have her head if she did anything to derail her plans. My hope for Novali to choose me over our mom's expectations at this moment is dashed. She is closer to Mom than I am. Mom is closer to her than she is to me. Novali is her golden daughter. If there is anyone who embodies everything this family stands for, it's Novali.

"Jazz will tell me the truth," I mumble as we leave the tea house.

"This is the truth. Marriage is work, and there is no doubt in my heart that you are going to kill it when it's your turn to walk down the aisle."

"Yayy!" I weakly cheer, and she elbows me.

"Jazz is going to tell you the same thing I told you."

"As his favorite little sister, he will tell me more."

She trips me as we get into the car, earning her a glare, which causes her to break out in laughter It's like an angel singing. The sound warms a cold corner of my heart. We should be together. That's how Nation families work. Wives and husbands marry into families, not away from them. Novali and her husband being in Paris for work is a sacrifice not typically made. We spent nearly every day of our lives together for our whole lives, and even with the years that have passed, my sister's absence is still felt.

When we return home, Mom is out at one of her friend's gatherings, which is a relief. Dad is sitting in his study. Not only had he taken to mom's family's work, but he kept his own family's ambitions going, especially with Chanson and Jazz. For a while, his pencil gliding across the paper keeps both of our attention.

"Darling, come in," he instructs without looking up.

Dad's welcome is already warm. His work is forgotten as I sit on his lap and examine his sketches.

"Where is this building going?"

"Alabama. Yonas is working with the local politicians to build a community center in one of the worst parts of the city. He commissioned us to do the project."

"That's huge, Dad."

"Jazz said the same thing. We have been working around the clock to make sure everything is right. Your mother is even helping with the eco part of the project."

"She has her hand in everything these days."

"Psalm..." he cautions.

"She's being insufferable."

"That's your mother," he adds, taking us to the balcony.

"Yes, and she is not concerned with mothering me right now."

"Psalm, you know you are more like me than all my other children."

"Meaning?"

"Meaning, when I was your age. I was stubborn, headstrong, and selfish. When it was time to grow up, it was time to grow up, and it is almost your time, princess."

"What about me is not grown up? The family doesn't pay my bills, dress me, or feed me. There is nothing I'm addicted to. Your daughter graduated top of her class *early*. I am healthy and happy. Isn't that enough?"

"For me? Of course, that was my only goal for you all growing up. However, that will never be enough for your mother and your people. You have a duty to your people. Every time you go to the biomes to find new ways to make things better for us, you are giving back to the community. But there is a more important way for you to give back."

"Through marriage?"

"That's what your mother says."

"What do you say?" I stress.

"Sir?" someone says, knocking on the door.

"Duty calls, princess. We have to wrap up this business before your mother gets home."

Well, since he won't answer my question, someone else will.

Jazz is sitting in the garden drinking his tea. For all of my life, he has been the most elegant man I've ever known. Even when we were little, his tunics were always in place, and his locs consistently crispy. He is clean down to his socks. As soon as he lays eyes on me, he hangs up the phone and pulls me into a hug.

"If it isn't my heart and soul."

"Jazz, please."

He holds me for a moment, making me feel so much better.

"What are you doing here? Dad went to work on that project."

"I'm leaving that to him today. Sherie is on her way with your nephew, and Mom will kill me if she catches me working."

"Do you love Sherie?"

"Of course, she is my wife."

"That doesn't mean you love her."

"Shouldn't it?"

"Things aren't always what they should be."

He examines me for a moment.

"In the beginning, it wasn't about love. She is a beautiful woman. We all know I'm fine as fuck. So I was down to see what kind of music we could make together. A fine ass bride was my one condition to Mom."

My eyes automatically roll.

"Plus, her family owns premium alternative energy, real estate, windmills, water-based energy, and all kinds of stuff. Mom wanted her hands on it."

"Are you kind to her?"

Jazz's face whirls in my direction. "Without a doubt. We love each other, and being good to the people I love is my number one priority. Are you worried about marriage?"

"Mom made some comments that make me think it's my time to get married. Mom and I don't see eye to eye anymore. We don't want the same things. She isn't going to pick the right one for me. Plus. there is nothing she has that I can't give myself."

"Wrong. I said the same thing, remember? There was nothing Mom could have offered me to get married, and suddenly there was. She knows you better than you know yourself. There will always be something you want that only she can give to you."

Jazz heads to grab his family, leaving me with my thoughts.

There is only one thing that could take my mind off things. Dad had built me a studio in our old garage not far from my room. He is always building things to get me to stay in LA. My eyes scan the record shelf until I find my favorite album, *Songs in the Key of Life*. Stevie's voice croons through the speakers as the materials come together. All of us had taken up weird hobbies. Something so off the wall that my mom wouldn't dare try to micro-manage. For me, it is doll making. It doesn't matter what kind. My favorites are the wooden ones. It takes a lot of time to carve them into perfect shape. The whittling knife works away delicate slices of wood as a face takes shape. I save the wooden ones for the girls who need them the most. It can take me a month or more to make one wooden doll. The plush ones take much less time.

When I started, it was to heal my inner child. Dolls were my favorite thing growing up, especially since mom made sure each doll looked exactly like us or the queen. For Mother's Day one year, we got a doll of her. My dolls listened to me more than anyone. They made me feel safe. My therapist told me to make a simple one, something to make me feel safe again. I'm still working on my inner child doll but the process, it's like an addiction. Sometimes, the process is the only thing to calm me down. That's the feeling I am chasing at this moment.

As the sun set, a final realization settles with me. Mom is planning on marrying me off. Marriage isn't high on my priority list. I don't care about getting married as long as my career comes first. Novali has chosen to be a complete housewife. Chyna is the opposite. She works more than the average Nation woman. My place is going to be somewhere in the middle. Being a housewife doesn't appeal to me. The work women do in the homes is extremely important, but that isn't my complete calling. Mom would lose her mind if those words left my lips out loud. Anyone who marries me will have to be comfortable with home being in Bali, and my work being first. We are so close to making a breakthrough that there is no way marriage is going to take me off the project.

"I knew you would be here," Chyna declares, leaning against the door frame.

We burst out into smiles and ran into each other's arms. Chyna and I are a different kind of close. She is my partner in crime and the one who gets in trouble with me. We were so bad together that Mom would separate us whenever we were together for too long. Dad calls us the troublemaker twins.

"I could have been anywhere."

"Yeah, but you make dolls when you're troubled, and I know why you feel troubled."

My tools clatter on the desk.

"No way Mom told you."

"She doesn't have to. My ear is to the ground. She wants you to get married."

"I thought so."

"Are you?"

"As long as I can stay in Bali, yes."

"That's your only condition?" she asks, baffled.

"Yup, I don't care about love, Chyna. I care about my work and my freedom."

"Love is important, too. You only get one shot at marriage, and you want to spend it with a random that mom chooses for you."

"I'll be fine. Novali is."

"She is not fine! Novali hates living in Paris, and with all the work Kocoum does, he barely has time for them. She would rather be home with us. Don't end up like Novali. Mom can't make you do anything. This is your life," she finishes.

"Oh, and dinner is ready. Make sure you wear what Mom laid out for you," she tosses over her shoulder.

Chyna is too young to understand. She hasn't even

graduated college yet. Yes, this *is* my life, but you don't go against the matriarch, and there has never been a time where she steered me wrong. Plus, getting married is a rite of passage, or duty, or our price for the life that we live. We are a community. If my family loses it all today, the Nation will support them, and their neighbors and friends will support them. We never have to face the big world alone, and for that, I would get married. For that, I would have a child. That is as far as it all went for me.

The pink and blue doll dress snags on my sewing machine, which signals that it's time for me to pack it up. Mom had to be having people over. There is no other reason for this urgency to come to dinner, not to mention the snugness of my abaya. I tied my head wrap tight, making sure not one of my thick curls are visible.

The table is packed when I make it downstairs. Mom had invited all of our family in town, and this is what it would be like until we wrap up the holiday season. Still, some of my favorite cousins are here, so sitting with them at the end of the table is *fun.* Jokes haven't flown like this in so long. There are few people my age who are doing work study in Bali, so it's nice to reconnect. The community there has gotten so small once my family moved back to the States. My maternal grandparents are all I had back in Bali, so this is refreshing. This is life-giving.

Chyna and I are cracking the most inappropriate jokes when Mom calls us to attention.

"Thank you, family, for coming to dinner tonight. Tomorrow, we officially begin Kwanzaa with Umoja, and what a way to begin by having my sisters, brothers-in-law, nieces, and nephews over for dinner. We truly appreciate you being here."

We all politely clap. I just want to get to the chicken and greens.

"Finally, we welcome my daughter Psalm back home to LA. Hopefully, this move becomes permanent once she finds a husband."

The table gasps.

"That's right, people. Psalm Jeladi Rose will be the next of my children to get married."

They cheer and pat me on the back. Only Chyna shares my worried glance.

Two

Soul

THE CLAY SITS in front of me untouched, as does my sketchbook. We are planning for show number four, which means I need to start working now. Every show has a theme. The last one was nature. I had sculpted soft leaves from stone, the arms, and elbows of Black people to show our oneness with nature. It was critically acclaimed. I don't know how to top the last show, but all of my ideas start with my sketchbook, and nearly nothing comes to mind. The panic I felt when I initially moved creeps into my mind.

"Any ideas?" Dad asks, putting his hand on my shoulder.

"Nothing," I reply.

"Your mother needs me to get our kinara and things out of storage. Want to come with me? It could clear your mind."

"Sure, let's go."

My skepticism aside, spending time with Dad again would

be nice. The longer New York is my home, the bigger the gap between us. We just want different things. We hauled all of Mom's decorations in the back of the SUV. At some point, I will get roped into decorating, too.

"We just have one more stop to make," he says.

Moments later, we arrive at the one place I don't want to be. The building is as imposing as always. The greenery covering most of it took the edge off, but it's still the same. Every hall is etched into my mind. Dad places his badge on the scanner, and people meet us as soon as we walk in.

"Soul, welcome back," someone said, shaking my hand.

I greet more people as we make our way to my father's office. As soon as he closes the door, he offers me a shot of Brandy. The glasses sing as we clink them and take the shot.

"Just like old times," I mutter.

Dad chuckles. "We could have those times again."

"Please, Dad."

"You're missing out on so much, son. Tech was your safe space. You used to love every corner of this place. Not to mention you are a genius at it. Hell, we are still using some of the semantics you drew in high school. What happened?"

The pressure happened. The weight of responsibility happened. His expectations happened.

"I just want to do something different."

"Soul, everything about you is different. You're the only man I know with a haircut."

"It's a partial. I still have locs."

"Barely," he scoffs before continuing. "Not to mention that septum piercing we fought your mom for."

That makes me burst out laughing, and he joins me. My

father's laughter is hearty and warm. I miss it. We have hardly laughed together since my move.

"Mom hated you for months after that."

"I have always gone to bat for you. When are you going to go to bat for me?"

"Soon, I have a few more shows in m—"

"What are you running from? LA would love to have you show your work here. Everything you love is here."

"I'm not running. I'm living."

"Living? You call your degeneracy in New York living? Have you fallen for a pagan woman?"

"No, you know that. I just need more time."

"I am running out of time. Soul, my retirement is almost upon me, and my legacy is in danger."

"Tade can—"

"It is not your brother's responsibility! It's yours! When are you going to grow the hell up?"

"I didn't ask for this!"

"No one asks for responsibility! Be a man and take your rightful place before I die!" he shouts.

"I'm out of here," I mumble.

This was bound to happen. Dad can't let me live for Soul and not for the Nation or the family. He gave his life to us, Mom, and his business, but I can't give up my life. I'm not ready yet.

Instead of going back to my studio at home, I went to Tree's home. His family is putting the icing on their decorations and are more than happy to have my help. All of their spare rooms are filled with family.

Tree has been my boy since diapers, except he is the grown-up. While I am working on my art, he has already taken over the family business and gotten married. His wife is pregnant with his first child as we speak, but he never pressures me to be anything other than myself. He always comes to my defense when the crew is on me about my life.

Once we are all done, his mother sends us away with some snacks and punch. We sit out on the back patio and watch them string up the last of the lights. The weight of my world crushed me for a moment, leaving tears in my eyes. My father's disappointment washes over me. Disappointing him is my biggest fear. I flinch when he is angry, anticipating the words he never says.

"Come on, let's meet up with the crew. They are at Diana's."

"Really? I thought we were all banned."

"Well, her mom says as long as we stay in the guest house, it's fine," Tree laughs.

The guest house is extravagantly done. Plush couches and warm curtains line the room inside, and the doors are thrown in to gaze at the beautiful water-laced view. We all managed to arrive at the same time. Diana pulls Kenji aside.

"The absolute first thing you need to do is take your ass in the house and apologize to my mother... again."

He groans but skips inside the house.

"It took a lot of begging to get my mom to let y'all back here. The least Kenji can do is grovel."

We laugh our way to the pool house, grabbing appetizers and drinks as we sit. It is early evening, which means the sky is blossoming with various colors, painting us in a golden hue.

The silence feels supportive and comforting. The dam inside

of me breaks. Hot tears soak my silk pants. Instinctively, they all move closer.

"It feels like there is no solution to this. My dad was so angry with me."

Juke hands me a tissue while Diana rubs my shoulders.

"What is your main conflict?" Tree asks.

"Taking over the family business feels like dying. Becoming my father's successor feels like a prison. You guys know Tech used to be my life. Hell, there was a time when all I wanted was to be the perfect Junior for him, but something changed in college. It felt like a metamorphosis. This is the Soul I like. In order to run the business, I would have to shift, but there is a part of me that still misses working with him, drawing semantics, and playing around with code."

"Soul, it's time for some tough love. Change isn't always a bad thing. It can bring you passions and pleasures you never thought you would get. Trust in Yah. Plus, you owe this to your people. They have given everything to you. It is time for you to give more back to them," Kenji comments.

"How do I make peace with change?"

"That is something you have to figure out and share these feelings with your father. He might be more understanding than you think," Xaevi adds.

"Well, now that we have that sorted. I say we go to Ezri's pre-Kwanzaa party," Tree says.

"No, there are always way too many people there," Diana dismisses.

"Look, tomorrow we are going to have people we haven't seen in *years* down our throat about shit that's not their business. There will be a limit on the bar and not a blunt in sight. At the very least, we can get trashed tonight and face the world tomorrow," Juke says, putting a foot on the table.

Diana shrugs. "Sold but get your foot off the table before Mom sees you!"

"I'm not sold," I voice.

"Shut up, Soul. No one asked you."

"Let's get fly," Tree says, rubbing his hands together.

Psalm

The floodgates of hell are open and out poured the people with question after question about shit that makes me uncomfortable. Thank Yah for Jazz. With a clink of his spoon on a glass, he ends all discussion about it. One thing Mom can't control is Jazz. He does whatever he wants and is consistently my saving grace. After the painful dinner, Chyna comes up to my room. She plays an imaginary trumpet complete with sound as Ezri prances through the door.

"The prince has arrived."

"More like the royal ass."

"Don't get snippy with me. It's time to get ready for my party."

"Ezri, you know damn well I am not going to that."

My declaration falls on deaf ears as he glides to my closet. It makes me smile a little. Ezri is the closest person to me outside of my family and makes it out to Bali several times a year to spend time with me. Nothing keeps us apart, and he is nearly half the reason I come back to LA a few times a year.

"Psalm, you won't dare break my heart like that. Plus, there is something I want to see you in. Novali brought it back from Paris for me."

He spends a while in my closet and comes out with a silk, gold abaya dress. The neckline is modestly scooped and completed by the heavy brown and gold silk embroidered abaya jacket. It is a heavenly fit and the perfect prelude to my Kwanzaa ensembles.

"Have Chyna help you get ready and be downstairs in an hour. I'm going to force Novali to come," he finishes before strolling out of the room.

Defeated, I take a shower before Chyna styles my hair in pretty loopy braids, adds the head wrap, and helps me get dressed. The silk makes a soft swish as it gently graces my feet. In the mirror, Chyna adds a little makeup in the form of gold eyeshadow, glitter, and nude lip.

"Ezri is right. We need to let our hair down tonight. Let's enjoy ourselves."

I can't agree more.

We all shuffle out of the house before Mom can question us.

There is a moderate chill in the air as we step out, signaling the arrival of California winter. Ezri's party has been one for the ages since we were in high school. Somehow, he knows what to have in order to relax everyone before the always exhausting and exhilarating holidays. It excites me to open my presents, light the kinara each night, win prizes, and hang out with my friends, but it wears me out too. Anticipation rushes into my lungs as I stick my head out of the sunroof.

"Woooooooo!"

Ezri laughs, and to my surprise, Novali sticks her head out the window. We scream together until I am teary-eyed. Ezri quickly dabs at my tears, careful of my makeup.

"Did that help?" he whispers.

A silent nod is my response, or the tears would slip out.

Thankfully, the car arrives at the castle-like mansion just outside of the community line. It is the best part of his party. Even Novali can let her hair down — there are no patrol cars, well-meaning aunties, or expectations. We are humans who are free, even if it is only for the night. Chyna drags us to the bar as soon as we walk in, and I allow myself to indulge.

"There is also a room for you in case you want to visit," Ezri suggests, wiggling his eyebrows.

We share a laugh before taking shots. Tonight is going to be a good night. It is determined to be.

Soul

"Aye, hit that shit!" Juke shouts as Kenji dances in the parking lot.

We may have pre-gamed too hard because now they both are dancing. Once Tree joins in, that is my cue to walk ahead of the pack. There is no way I am dancing like that in these satin slacks and corduroy tunic. The light hit the only two gold chains I wore, then my gold pinky ring. I opt for solid gold fangs and a re-twist to seal the look. Yeah, I am definitely leaving the dancing to them.

Diana is just as pretty as I am and is also determined to keep it that way, so she is steering clear of the rowdy boys. Xaevi gazes at the stars for a moment. In his posture, I understand what he is saying. This feels *fun*. It feels like youth, irresponsibility, and blessings. When his gaze meets mine, he smiles, knowing he is heard. Once we get inside, Diana takes on her usual role as pusher.

"Shots, shots, shots!" She cheers, sliding them across the bar to us.

"What are we toasting to?" Kenji asks.

"My wedding?" Diana questions.

"A night we won't remember?" I suggest.

"To both," Tree decides as we start a long night of shots.

It turns out this party has changed drastically. There are so many people I haven't seen in years, old friends, and some I met in New York. The food is amazing, and it absorbs the alcohol Diana keeps pushing on us. Kenji forces me into the smoke room and laughs at the expression on my face. Smoking isn't for me, especially since it doesn't take much to get me lifted, which is proven in the literal next minute. Kenji pushes me through the rest of the house, and somehow Tree gets ahold of me. He puts a controller in my hand, leading me to fight for my life in FC. He scores a goal on me, and the crowd goes wild, making me laugh uncontrollably. Tears slip out of the corner of my eyes as Tree hits me with a glance. I haven't felt this light in a long time. I'm not worried about topping my last exhibit or bending under Dad's pressure. At this moment, my best friend is whooping my ass in soccer, and it's hilarious.

Psalm

"Chyna, on three. One. Two."

We both toss back a shot of gin and giggle. Novali and Ezri are dancing to Drake. She looks so free at this moment. There is even a hint of her escaping curls under her head wrap. The ease in the air causes me to notice the sister on my right. Chyna is long past drunk and starts pushing me to the dance floor. We dance and twirl to the music as a group and then back in pairs. I am laughing so much my cheeks hurt. The liquor is causing the room to be blurry.

"Smoke!" Chyna shouts in my ear, dragging me in the direction of the smoke room.

"Hold up," I try but am drowned out by the music.

Chyna grabs my forearm and pulls me in her direction. My feet can hardly keep up.

"Girl, slow down!" I shout.

Soul

Tree scores another goal, causing the crowd to chant his name.

"Thanks for the confidence boost, everybody," I sarcastically state.

A goal comes from me out of nowhere, and I throw my hands up in excitement, flipping off the crowd.

Suddenly, a shadow looms over me.

Psalm

A couch appears out of nowhere. Chyna dodges it but must have forgotten she is holding on to a person. I crash into the couch and…

Three

Soul Niwibwe

SHE FALLS right into my arms. Instinctively, I hold on to her. Those wide chocolate brown eyes lock onto mine. My heart skips a beat. I am immediately confident that in every world I got to gaze into these eyes. The warmth from her gentle frame oozes throughout the chambers of my heart.

What is this feeling?

She smirks at me. The gentle upturn of her glossed lips conveys simple elegance. I am at a loss for words.

"Yah must have me given my gift early."

"If you consider me a gift, you must have been bad this year." She flirts.

"On the contrary, I've been well-behaved, seeing as there is an angel in my lap."

She surprises me by rolling her eyes. "If that's the best you can do, I'll be getting up now."

A woman reaches out for her. A cascade of gold silk envelopes her for a moment, framing her delicate features as she stands. I watch her adjust her head wrap and scold the woman who helped her up.

My wit returns.

"Oh, so you're mean to everybody."

Even the wrath she turns on me is charming and flirtatious

"Stern, not mean, and judging by the haircut and piercing, you need more sternness."

"Not an insult to my mother." I mock being wounded.

"On the contrary, the insult is towards the one embarrassing her as a son."

"I hope that means you're volunteering to teach me more manners."

"Not on your life," she scoffs.

The woman she is with pulls her away, leaving me in awe.

Psalm

I should be sleeping, knowing the night we had, but it escapes me. Instead, my stomach is calling for breakfast. That man is on my mind as well. He is so handsome and managed to catch me before my body slid off his lap. His smile is stuck in my mind, too. He is witty. I should have at least gotten his name. Chyna is at the kitchen sink when I stroll in.

"Now that you're up, help me with breakfast." She pushed pancake ingredients in my direction.

"Don't you have a husband to annoy?"

"Abraham is with his family this morning. We will see each other later tonight, so I am here to annoy you instead."

She declares giving me a cup of coffee for encouragement.

"Who was that guy holding you last night?" she quizzed suggestively.

"He wasn't holding me. I fell into his lap because *someone* wasn't watching where she was going."

She rolls her eyes as Novali enters the kitchen, starting on the eggs.

"Looks like he was holding her to me."

"Chyna basically pushed me."

"That's the story we'll tell Mom," Chyna chuckles, stealing a blueberry.

"Honestly, I don't know who that man is."

"Well, he is cute," Novali adds.

"The man Mom picks for her will be cute enough," Chyna sarcastically says.

Uh oh. This was going to cause some issues.

"He will be. Kocoum is," Novali obliviously replies.

"Kocoum also leaves you and a nanny to raise your children, right? Is that what you want for Psalm?"

"Okay, let's talk about the ugliest dress I've ever seen or discuss the rumors about the queen to be swirling Jiacom?" I suggest.

"No, Chyna, I want Psalm to have everything she wants. I trust Mom will give those things to her."

"Like she gave them to you? What was your condition? Money?" Chyna snaps.

"It was for security and prosperity. We can't all be like you," Novali spat.

"Ladies, breakfast," I try again.

"You're upset because I found love and money. Maybe you could have found it too if you weren't so eager to be Mom's lapdog!"

"That is *enough!*" I shout, causing both of them to be silent.

"We made a promise to enjoy the holiday season together. There will be no bickering about my potential marriage. It ends right here. Right now!"

Chyna and Novali share a worried glance.

"Now make the damn eggs and turkey sausage!"

We continue making breakfast, the mood shifting by the time Mom enters the kitchen. Nothing is going to ruin Kwanzaa this year, not even sibling bickering.

"Thanks for giving me a head start. Your aunt kept me out late last night." She pauses, taking in the room. "What's the matter with you girls?"

"Pre-unity party jitters," I offer before they could speak.

Mom doesn't pry and helps us with breakfast. Once everyone else is up. The mood truly goes back to normal. Sherie and Jazz kiss then plop my nephew down in his highchair. The table is full to the brim, and we are laughing again. Someone puts on Kwanzaa music.

There are no prying or difficult conversations. It is all skiing trips, assignments, and holiday breaks. Everyone is smiling, but Chyna and Novali's argument echo in my ears. There is worry sweeping through my heart. I don't want to be stuck halfway around the world with just my children or not allowed to chase my dreams. Nation women have a lot of freedom, but a lot of restrictions. The best way is to find a partner who loves the things you love. You often find a traditional match, especially with our status, someone who wants you to only work in approved fields and focus on the home. Other times, you get lucky.

Chyna is lucky. She and Abraham became best friends in primary school. They were just as tight as Ezri and I were. Except once they were in high school, they fell in love. Abraham's family owns all the farms in Paris, so of course, my mother wanted access to those, too. She is collecting connections like infinity stones. Mom went along with what Chyna wanted because she loved Abraham's family. They had something she wanted, and she knew Chyna would be loved with them. Mom's family didn't start in this level of society. Her mother matched her daughters strategically to change their lives. Mom has followed her lead in that regard. The connections she collects are everything. There are plenty of families who want in. A part of me is scared she will find someone who isn't like me. All for the sake of a connection needing to be made. It is hard to trust her, and we haven't talked since the night she announced me being on the market. Every time she looks at me, I look away. There is nothing for us to discuss. She has made my choice for me, but pretty soon, I would have to bite the bullet and talk to her.

———

Once we are getting dressed for the party, my mom comes to help, which means she wants to talk.

"I knew this green would look great on you."

"Because you know everything."

"Psalm, be fair. I only want to ensure you and this family are taken care of. You know, I thought Chyna would be the difficult one."

"Yah spared you and sent her Abraham."

She laughs, but I don't.

"Name your condition, and I'll meet it."

It can't be a simple condition. I have to choose something Mom would never give me.

"Bali, and my work. That is my condition. If you want me to get married, my work and Bali come first."

"Done. Now you should wear your grandmother's emerald choker tonight. I'll go get it."

She didn't fight me. Mom always fought me — during prayer time, when I started wearing head wraps, and dinner time. We were at odds numerous times in my life. We are supposed to be at odds right now. This is the one thing I thought she was going to fight me on, but as Jazz said, Mom always knows what you want more than anything.

Gratefully, it is just the family at this party tonight. There are no potential suitors and moms to smile for, just the family. Umoja is the first day of Kwanzaa. It's all about celebrating family, togetherness, and unity, so for the first day, we always gather as a family.

The size of our tribe is apparent to me as I watch them drive in.

"Psalm, it's time for us to go down," Jazz says, adjusting his black tunic.

There is no doubt in my mind that word has traveled about my mom's goals for me. They will have a thousand questions about it. About me, and with Novali and Jazz being married with children and Chyna being married at all, there is usually enough excitement that keeps me off their minds, but now everything will be on me.

"Palm, it's time for us to go," Jazz says gently, using my childhood nickname.

"They are going to devour me," I whisper back.

"You know I'm not going to let that happen. Sherie won't either."

"You guys can't be my shadows all night."

"Then let us be your lighthouse," he offers, pulling me off the balcony. He kisses my forehead and adjusts my head wrap before grabbing my hand.

As soon as we step out of my room, we are greeted by a roar of noise. A glance over the balcony shows me a wash of abayas. All in varying shades of red and green. All the men are in inky black tunics of varying designs. We look like a waving Pan-African flag. We look like unity.

"Tonight is going to be painless. You won't even remember it," Jazz whispers as we walk down the stairs.

My gut is telling me he will be wrong. Novali pushes her way through the crowd, and by the look on her face, I can tell she has been looking for us.

"There you are. Mom is waiting for us to make the introduction speech. You two are the only ones missing."

Novali doesn't wait for our response. She just takes off expecting me to follow. Jazz is struggling to keep up. Mom is standing at the head of the room, surrounded by our family. Every spouse is up there too. Mom hits us with a glare for being late when no one is watching.

After twenty agonizing minutes, the room is finally full to her liking.

"Attention, attention. Thank you, family and friends, for coming out to celebrate the first day of Kwanzaa with us," Mom begins.

"Many of you were also at my and my wife's wedding. You were here for every child we added along the way. All of you make up the great family I was blessed enough to marry and be born into. As we light the first candle in the kinara, know that you all are a part of every flicker of the flame. Thank you for welcoming every new spouse and grandchild. Thank you for always being here and for the many years of Unity to come. To Umoja!" Dad finishes with a shout.

"To Umoja!" they all shout back.

Their voices are uplifting and encompassing. The strength and size of our family never cease to leave me in awe. The rest of the immediate family scramble away from my mother, and I try to do the same, but she catches me.

"Let's see the room," she whispers, dragging me to the last people I want to see.

My mom walks us over to the group of aunties from both sides. The hunger in their eyes clearly palpable, like they have been waiting for this moment.

"Valencia, this is an amazing party. You all have outdone yourselves," my dad's sister, Jalani, offers.

"It couldn't have been done without your brother and the children. We all worked hard to put this party together for the family."

"Not Psalm, though. She was doing 'better' things in Bali. Right Psalm?" my mom's sister, Clara, asks.

"There was some delay in me coming home, but more than enough work left for me."

Mom had lost the reins as soon as Aunt Clara opened her mouth.

"So, will you be moving back to LA, seeing as you're on the marriage market now?"

"She doesn't have to leave Bali to get married," Mom interjects, causing the group to scoff in unison.

"Please, Valencia. How could she stay? Once the majority of the community moved back, we thought everyone would, but here is Psalm and her stubborn grandmother holding on," one adds.

"In order to be a successful wife, Psalm must be in America and LA."

Before Mom can answer, a crisis pulls her away. She almost takes me with her, but they keep me talking.

"Psalm, we have recommendations, but you will have to make adjustments."

"Adjustments?"

"Scaling back your work hours is a great start. How are you supposed to care for your husband and his family if you are always working?"

"Auntie, do you know what I do?"

"Does it matter?" Aunt Jalani asks.

"Of course it does. It is my job to make sure all of our ecosystems are balanced. Controlled fires in LA, and soil replacement in Morocco. It takes a lot of work to get done."

"That's more important to you than finding a husband and having children?"

"Making sure our farms can feed every man, woman, child, and pet in the Nation is desperately important."

"Psalm, your mother needs your help with dinner. I'm sorry for stealing her ladies, but we all can agree that she needs as much practice as she can get."

They laugh at my expense, and an elbow from my dad prompts me to laugh, too. A nervous laugh escapes my lips as he pulls me away.

"What does Mom need my help with?" I asked once we were out of earshot.

"Nothing. You were drowning and a few words away from swinging, so I had to interrupt."

We share a hug. His warm embrace almost brings me to tears. Dad is always my hero, and now, more than ever, he is here when I need him the most.

"Take a deep breath and clear your head. You have allies out here. Do the work and find them. Psalm, I love you, but you are moving like a quitter. Who has the most power over you?"

"Yah."

"Who else?"

"Me."

"Act like it."

He pats my shoulder, and before he leaves me, his eyes catch on a few people. That is my cue. Although Dad never contradicts our mother, he does not bow to her. He works in tandem with her, and in time, you can see he is the one in charge. The founding principle of our childhood has been our autonomy. We answer to Yah and no one else. We owe respect to everyone else unless our autonomy is threatened. Right now, mine is being threatened.

The people on whom his eyes linger are indeed allies. They understand the importance of my work and want to align me with matches that will fit the criteria for the family. I had forgotten that included me. Mom is not in charge of this marriage. I am. The final decision is on me. Dad has reminded me of my power, and so has Chyna. This marriage season doesn't have to be tricky. It can be mine.

Soul

"Soul, check on dinner, and for the love of Yah, put on presentable clothes," Mom chastens.

For a moment, it's like being thirteen again. Unity parties never fail to amaze me. We have at least a hundred people comfortably in this home. Each person familiar to me in their way. The connection between us is like a web of support, and the love is vast, stretching out to reach me no matter how far I go. Us being together is like a constant celebration, not to mention the gifts. They give me food, money, and things I like and don't like. You never know what you are going to get. Those times were nothing like my last Unity party. My uncles said some harsh words to me. It led to me dismissing myself from the party early. This year, I won't be so easily moved.

I wore black per tradition, but there was a Soul spin on it. My tunic was made almost a year ago. The darkest silk was used for the tunic, and the darkest leather used for the pants. I put in my gold and black diamond septum ring. My gold fangs and my grandfather's chains complete the look. This is nothing but money, baby. It's refinery. They will find a grown man in front of them this time. Dinner is on schedule, so I tuck myself away for a little while. There is still nothing in my sketchbook. It's rare to find me without inspiration. Dad taught me that art is all around us, and only the real could see it. My ability to see art in everything was Yah's first gift to me. It makes creating easy. My stagnancy is frustrating.

"Hey Casanova, the party is going to start soon. Parents want pictures," Tade says.

"Oh no, what have you heard?"

"You had a hottie in your lap, and you were flirting," Isra

answers.

"Here? You guys are mad. I would never disrespect a Nation woman like that."

"Oh, pagan pussy is okay, but Yah forbid a Nation woman falls in your lap."

"See, that's the terminology we need. She fell into my lap, and I made sure she didn't fall further."

"You're such a gentleman," Isra mocks.

"You mock me, but it's true. A Nation woman's honor is always in the highest regard in my presence."

"Anyway, we heard she put your ass in your place." Tade laughs.

"Fake news. We exchanged brief words. Again, nothing that would make anyone worry." I defended.

"She definitely put you in your place. That's a PR statement."

We laugh our way into the foyer.

"Soul, that is a beautiful tunic. This haircut ruins your look I wish you would grow your hair out," Mom tsks, adjusting my locs.

"Maybe when I'm old."

Dad comes down the stairs next. We haven't spoken since I left the office. He used to be so big to me. We had grown to be the same height, but he still had a couple of pounds on me.

"Nice to see you're still taking style cues from your old man." He laughs.

We shake hands, and he hugs me briefly — a truce for the night.

"You know I had to put my spin on it."

We share another laugh before Mom shoos us away to our stations. Thankfully, she puts me behind the scenes to ensure we have enough glasses, and the music is at the right volume.

That's fine by me. You talk to fewer people behind the scenes. Since I am a mama's boy, she is always going to protect me, and keeping me out of the fray is the best way to do that. Unfortunately, that can't last for long.

"Soul! Come over here and have a word with us, boy."

For the love of Yah.

"Uncle, how was Morocco?"

"Brief, the way a vacation is supposed to be."

Here he goes.

"Of course, because who has time for long vacations?"

The group laughs which feels natural, but my uncle does not take the cue.

"You seem to have all the time in the world for them. Seeing you have been in New York for quite a while," he scolds.

"If it were a vacation, everyone would know. New York is all about work. I am three solo shows in and working on my fourth."

"The arts are all fine and dandy, but when they take you away from your real responsibilities, then it's a problem."

"What responsibilities are those?" I ask, swirling my whisky in its cold glass.

"Soul, that attitude will not be tolerated this time around. While you are playing around in New York, your father is working his ass off."

"He's not the only one."

"Art isn't work," he retorts.

"Yes, it is."

"If so, it isn't what's most important. You have a duty to your father and your people."

"Dad is not senile. We are scheduling my time as future CEO."

"Bullshit. You're not even married yet. You just spend all your time floating around New York while real shit is happening in real-time."

Soul, keep calm.

It's time for me to be on business.

"Look, I understand you have a unique investment in this company, but this matter is between Dad and me. Now, we shouldn't talk about work at a Unity party. Please, enjoy."

I toss back the rest of my whisky and discard the cup on a passing tray. Mom would murder me and put me on the menu if a scene were made on my behalf. It would be on me to control the narrative and a bunch of other things she's said that are forgotten to me. It is in my eventual best interest to walk away. My uncle doesn't want any smoke with my mom either.

There is solace out in the garden, and not many people are out here. Most of them are inside, listening to my mom singing at the piano. The sound of the keys seep out with the ballroom lighting. For a moment, the music takes hold of me. It takes the tension out of my back. The sound of Whitney Houston's notes comes out of the house on a gentle breeze. She is the only pagan artist my mom allows in the house.

For some reason, this song reminds me of that woman from the party. When she fell into my arms, her energy gathered all of my attention. Before our eyes met, she already had me enraptured. It was silent for the first time in my life. Not the kind of silence that makes you seek others or turn up the music. No, it's the kind of silence you seek all your life. It's peace. As soon as her body left mine so did warmth. Her name, her name. We should have at least exchanged names, something to keep me tied to the moment for even a second longer. My siblings are right that she put me in my place. Nation women do not challenge, scold, or quip at you. They are pious and delicate. At most, an average Nation woman would have giggled or walked away. Normally, I wouldn't have flirted, but that is the power of weed and alcohol.

If all Nation women were like that, it would have been easier for me to settle down. There is so no desire in me for a servant, a yes woman, or someone who makes lamb for dinner every night and gets us to service on Sundays. It feels as constricting as taking over does. Of course, Yah is the head of my life. I don't celebrate major holidays or buy from non-Black establishments, but maybe I don't make it to see my shaman every Sunday, or I speak more English than Hebrew. Having a replica of my mom breathing down my neck about the little things is more stress than I need, so we established a long time ago that marriage is not a high priority for me. That is made more evident by my move to the East Coast. Honestly, it is amazing that they didn't cut me off and we still have a great relationship.

Someone hands me a glass of whiskey, and I take it.

"Carlo chewed you out, huh?" Dad asks.

"Without a doubt."

"You did better than you did last year," he offers.

There is no more polite laughter in me.

"Soul it's going to be okay. I know you better than anyone else does. One day, you will be ready. I just hope it's someday soon."

"How do you know when you are ready?"

"You don't ever know. It's a leap of faith, son."

Dad slaps me on the back a couple of times and heads back inside for the party. The whiskey slides down my throat in a comforting burn. Mom's voice carries my name on the breeze. It is time to go back to pretending.

Four

Psalm

JAZZ IS WRONG. I will never forget last night's party. It represents my life in more ways than I am ready to admit. There is always duty on my heels, grabbing at the curls under my head wrap, threatening me. Then there is the rest of it — the joy, being smothered with love by the cousins I only see once a year, lighting the kinara with my family, stealing wings from Jazz's plate, and singing with Chyna. It was an amazing party. It makes me look forward to everything that is coming up next.

Thankfully, we have more personal Kwanzaa events than formal ones, which means most of these events will be with my peers. It takes the weight off my shoulders and would make things much more enjoyable. It is day two. Kujichagulia is all about defining ourselves. The Nation makes a name for itself in many ways. We define ourselves in many ways. Yah is an integral part of who we are as a people, so we typically start day

2 with a service from our shaman. Mom woke everyone bright and early for service.

Novali helps me into my burgundy abaya, laughing at my zombie-like state.

"I know you didn't party this hard."

"You didn't see how many shots I had behind Mom's back."

Our laughter rings toward the ceiling.

This is the most silent we have been in an eternity. The shuffling of our feet, the only noise in the crisp morning. Sunlight is barely peeking over the treetops, and a fog is settling in the distance. This is the type of twilight words can spoil. The church looms over us. The white walls stretch overhead. This church has been my home whenever we weren't in Bali, so stepping into the adorned space is relaxing. Jazz's shoulders straighten. Novali's boys settle down, as they gaze upon the stained glass and frescos that enrich the walls.

Yah's melanated people leave me in awe every single time. They are beautiful just like he is. That man from the party. He is breathtaking, handsome, and gentle. I bet his name is sweet. Dad shuffles to our usual pew space. As we settle in, my eyes drift over the crowd. There he is. Looking up at the frescos. His full lips grew a smirk. Blue light drew highlights across the well-cut thickness of his beard. My body gravitates towards my seat as my eyes continue tracing the richness of his skin down to the scandalous pecs peeking out o his tunic, glistening in the early sunlight. My eyes never left his patient frame. I want to walk over and take his hand. My heart flutters as he strolls towards his pew.

What is this feeling?

The choir wakes us up with a Kwanzaa-centered number that gets us on our feet. Soon, we are all up praising and worshiping the foundation of our well-being. The one who makes all of this possible every day. The Almighty Yah. Still, my eyes haven't forgotten his skin glowing in the natural light from the ceiling. It feels authentic. Like holding his hand would silence all the noise in my head.

By the time the shaman takes the pulpit, the room is lively. The angels have heard our praise. Shaman Chukwu's hand waving over the crowd sits us down. He speaks of blessings, responsibility, and prosperity.

"Remember, ladies and gentlemen, Yah is who you owe your loyalty to. Committing to his laws and ways will propel you into a life of comfort. Be steadfast. Never waver from his love."

Shaman Chukwu's voice vibrates through the hollow hall. Conviction blossoms in my chest. My fear of the future shrinks. I owe Yah and my people a union. I owe them the future. Chyna grips my hand as we exit the church. There he is again. His long body leaned under the dangling peach trees. An ache to run my fingers through his locs washes over me.

"Psalm, we're going out for breakfast. Are you coming?" Chanson asks.

"Yeah, sure.", I reply, finally tearing my eyes away from the tree.

Later that night, we hire a few babysitters, and the crew gets ready to go. Kenji, one of the most famous authors of our generation, is hosting a poetry slam. Kujichagulia is all about declaring yourself, your beliefs, and your personality. It celebrates the Black community's creativity and self-determination. Kenji's poetry slam is the perfect place to do that.

"Psalm, Psalm," Chyna calls, pulling me out of my thoughts. "Did you write something?" she presses.

"Of course, it would be a lost opportunity if not. What about you?"

"Hell no. I plan to secretly get drunk in the back and listen to everyone else."

"That's not fair. Where is your Kujichagulia spirit?"

"You have enough for both of us. Help me."

She motions toward her eyes and gives me the mascara tube. Gentle silence stretches between us as I finish her modest makeup.

"Abraham, doesn't mind you coming out with us? Where is he?"

"Nope, he says I am free to hang out with you for as long as I want."

"Whatever. It's odd how few family events they are hosting."

"His mom said something about taking things easier this year. She is getting old."

"That means you'll have to be the family matriarch."

"As if."

"You did marry her oldest son, Chyna."

"*Anyway*, is Jazz coming with us?"

"No, but Novali is," I answer, applying my lip gloss.

Chyna flops down in the chair beside me.

"Please don't behave that way. She is your sister, and you love her."

"Of course, but that doesn't make me like her archaic views."

"You don't have to like them, but you do have to respect them. Sometimes you show your age, Chyna."

She sneers at me before going back to her room.

It isn't easy being the middle child. At times, you are the

most forgotten. With Jazz and Novali being the perfect older children and my youngest siblings requiring all the attention in the world, I was often left alone, so unless I made a fuss, no one paid attention to me besides my father. It was even worse within our sibling dynamic until I turned sixteen. Now, it is all about being the voice of reason — stopping Chyna and Novali from fighting, replacing Jazz's cologne that Chanson stole. One of us has to keep the peace, and I don't mind being that person.

"Yo," Chanson says before plopping down on my beanbag chair.

"What do you want?"

"Mom says I'm coming with you tonight."

"As if. Jazz isn't going to be there, so that means you aren't either."

"Jazz is going, and so is Sherie, which means you're taking your brother," Mom said, giving me a dress bag.

"Mom, come on!"

She ignores me, and Chanson gives me a smug smile.

"Get out."

"I'll be ready soon," he calls as he leaves.

This would be the first time all five of us would go out together. Since Chanson had just turned eighteen, he was finally allowed to come out with us. We would get a break from all his complaining about being left behind. In my eyes, he is still my baby brother. How are we supposed to turn up with him here? Jazz will be trying to set an example for Chanson like always, which means he would be no fun, and with all the beef between Chyna and Novali, this is shaping up to be a not-so-good night.

Since all the doors to my suite are now locked, I had the privacy to get dressed. Gratefully, this is a peer event, there is no need to wear a traditional abaya. A long white turtleneck slip dress covered in a sky-blue skirt and abaya jacket gave off the appearance of traditionalism while maintaining comfort. Every movement made caused the sky-blue material to swish around my ankles. Mom was not happy when I made it down the stairs.

"Psalm, what in Yah's name are you wearing?"

"An abaya."

"Please, those are barely modest pieces."

"Honey, she looks amazing, and she's going to be with all of her friends, anyway. Get your coat and let the kids enjoy Kwanzaa."

Dad kissed my cheek and did the same for my sisters as he and Mom headed out the door. Jazz came down the stairs alone, surprising us.

"Where is Sherie?" Chyna asked.

"She's staying with Junior. Tonight's Chanson's initiation." Jazz's teeth showed blinged-out fangs. He only wore them when he was in the mood for trouble.

The mood immediately picked up. Kenji is hosting just on the edge of our property, and the coffee shop is already brimming when we arrive. The noise is comforting. It made me feel like we were in high school again. All we had to worry about was being ourselves. Jazz was already gathering shots enough for all of us to take two. That made Chanson's eyes go wide.

"Who that's for?"

"You! Get ready to see a different side to your brother!" Novali shouted over the music.

We did our limes and salt before taking the shots. We laugh at Chanson's scowl. Pretty soon, Kenji graced the stage.

"Yah knows that man is fine," Chyna whispers.

Novali's eyes lower in contempt, but my glare keeps her silent.

"Ladies and gentlemen, please direct your attention to the stage."

He patiently waits for the crowd to settle down. His energy had a calming edge to it.

"Welcome to Kujichagulia. Welcome to the celebration of who you all are. Identity is the foundation of our community. It is what shapes us and molds us. Yah is your foundation, and your love for your people is the heavy bricks that make up each floor of our house. One by one, your peers will show you what our community's identity looks like. Thank you. Reflect and enjoy." He bows as we snap.

The first woman strolls out on stage. The lights drop, and she performs a beautiful piece about love in all of its forms. Chyna supplies us with shots as more and more people say their piece. It was beautiful. As Kenji promised, we got to see our community.

"Next up, Soul Niwibwe," someone announces.

There is the man from Ezri's party. He is breathtaking. The lighting on the stage proves that he looks good anywhere. Soul's body moves with gentle confidence. There is no arrogance in his steps. He takes his time walking up the mic, and we are all captivated as he moves. Whoa, I have never felt anything like this before. This emotion I'm feeling is un-placeable. Soul's voice amplifies my feelings.

"Thank you for that riveting introduction."

The crowd chuckles. Soul closes his dark eyes for a moment, then begins.

A curve as gentle as snow when the sun first shines.

The turn opens to new light, new beginnings.
The heart lays carefully on the ice.
Red.
Dripping,
Exposed to the sun's dark rays.
On the outside, it is grotesque, but on the inside, it is blessed.
Yah lays his hand on the veins and ventricles.
Making something new.
Something real.

I feel like he is looking at me even though he isn't.

"I thought our poem was supposed to be about ourselves," Chyna comments.

"His was," I whisper back.

We shared the same emotions. The same place in life. He is trapped just like me.

"Next up, we have Psalm Rose."

Soul

Song Flower. She couldn't have a more fitting name. Her body moves like easy waves as she takes the stage. Everyone goes quiet naturally. It is like her aura passed through the crowd. I have never felt more relaxed. *What kind of woman is this?*

"Thank you everyone. This piece is foundationally Psalm."

Her eyes are drawn to her friends. The woman from the party gives her a thumbs up.

Darkness covers below and underground.

There is not a word, no softening or sound.

Who are we when we are below, when we mix with the things we don't know?

What if we could push against the darkness?

What if we curved with our fears and drowned with our sorrows?

If we stopped counting tomorrows?

Light, glorious, wet, and cold light.

It fills you, it pushes you, it consumes you until cooled by the white waters.

Until your shape is familiar.

Until you are someone.

"She looks familiar. Her poem was interesting..." Diana comments.

"Indeed," I voice.

For a moment, we locked eyes. I expect Psalm to be hard towards me like she was at the party, but there is a delicacy in her gaze. Once she finishes, we stay in a trance for what feels like forever. Once she walked off, her absence on the stage was felt immediately. It doesn't matter who walks out next or where we go after. She is the only person on my mind.

"Who is she?" I blurt while we are getting cheeseburgers downtown later.

"Who?" Xaevi asks, confused.

"Psalm, of course," Diana answers, rolling her eyes.

"Oh, she caught your eye, huh?" Kenji teases.

"Of course, her piece was interesting. Is she a writer?" I fish.

"No, a botanist. She's never in LA, though," Diana answers.

"Why?"

"Bali is where she does most of her work. She's here a few times a year to collect samples, and you are the last man she would ever talk to," Juke adds.

"What's wrong with me?"

"Let's start with the fact that you don't live in LA and your love for… philandering," Kenji asserts.

"That doesn't mean I'm not worthy of love."

Kenji laughs, and Diana rolls her eyes.

"Of course you are, but you aren't ready, especially for a woman like her," Diana says seriously.

Who are they to tell me what I am ready for?

"We can tell you because we know you," Tree interjects, reading my mind.

When I get back home, it is almost morning time. Sleep isn't going to have time to find me tonight. My friends' comments are still on my mind while the steam from the shower creates a comforting fog around me.

There is no question about my eligibility. My father is a tech giant, and my mother is a renowned chef. Both families are highly respected. My yearly salary would make some people's eyes water, and I am a Yah-fearing man. I am the total package. Right? Psalm would be more than happy to have a man like me. Right? Or maybe things had changed around me without me realizing it.

Tade was already on his way down for breakfast when we met on the stairs.

"Shouldn't you be asleep?"

"There is no point. Do you think I'm marriage material?"

His eyebrows came together in confusion.

"Since when do you give a damn about that?"

"Since right now. So am I?"

"No, you are not," Isra answers, coming down the stairs.

"What?"

She got serious.

"Soul, we love you more than anything. Any woman would be lucky to have you when you are ready. At this time, you aren't ready to be a Nation husband."

Tade's solemn expression told me agreed with Isra, and they went down to breakfast without me. For some reason, I thought it would be easy for me to waltz back in and get married when the occasion came up. It never occurred to me that there would be a lack of available brides.

"Soul, are you okay?" Mom asks.

My eyes were trained on my plate for nearly the entire breakfast. Any time they tried to involve me, it didn't last very long.

"He was out all night for day two. Tade is surprised he's still standing," Dad answers for me.

Once breakfast is wrapped up, we have some time to kill before day three activities.

So, I head to the Nation Gardens. Everyone is out in full force and Tree plans on meeting me there with his wife. I haven't had much time to get to know her. Tree is going to spend Ujima with us, so we won't see Alena later. Everyone is out in the gardens today. Steam rises from the tea cups going around on the carts. Frost decorates some of the rose bushes. A woman not too far away is trying to lift a bag of mulch.

My hands catch it before it slips from her polished fingers.

"Thank you, these bags are heavier than I thought."

Psalm's Hebrew is so formal, I nearly don't understand it.

"No problem. I always help a woman in need."

I help her load up the rest of the bags. Her directions are clear and concise. There is no room for misunderstanding, except language-wise.

"Let me treat you to some tea. It's the least I can do." She suggests. Psalm's gaze is captivating in a flirtatious way. It leaves my mouth dry.

"Of course, but only if we give it a rest with the formal Hebrew."

Her laugh is slightly condescending as she approaches the vendor. There is something she is hiding or holding back.

"So, I was right then,?"

I take the teacup from her hand. "About?"

"You needing sternness, your Hebrew is…lacking."

"Please don't fault me. I am just out of practice. Maybe you have time to re-educate me."

"If you ask nicely, I'll consider it." She bites her tongue, smiling cheekily.

My heart skips a beat as we stare into each other's eyes. They are like whirlpools. Each second gazing into them sent me deeper towards the secrets of her heart.

"Soul!" Tree calls, pulling me out of her trance.

"I'll be waiting." She whispers before sauntering away.

My, my, my.

"We've been looking for you forever." He scolds.

"I'm sorry I got carried away with something. Alena. Tree talks about you all the time."

"Then we have something in common." She jokes.

I don't let go of the teacup Psalm gave to me. It could be all in my head, but it feels like her fingers are still on it. Trying to pay attention is difficult. Psalm won't leave my mind. The curve of her hips, perfect Hebrew, and polite nature towards everyone she meets made me feel… well I can't even find the words.

Tree and Alena don't keep me long. I feel bad that this is my first time having a long conversation with her. At the wedding, we didn't get a word in with each other. In fact, the only thing we had time for was a quick hello. I missed their coming out and engagement party, because of art. I'm grateful Tree and Alena don't hold it against me. The house is nearly empty when I return. Since there is no one looking over my shoulder, I can do some digging. My encounter with Psalm made me too curious not to find out more about her.

I am going to find out why my friends thought so highly of the Song Flower. My first step is looking into Nation botany. Logically, I know they exist, but the amount of work they do for all our communities is astonishing — managing all our farms, ensuring the natural lawn biomes are safe, and starting and maintaining natural forests across all of our lands. Five families manage the system together, which makes Pslam more impressive.

Multiple families regularly maintain particular career fields to ensure we are comfortable in all aspects. Fifty families ensure our education systems run smoothly, and one hundred families manage all of our grocery stores. Of course, the more serious the job, the fewer hands on deck. There are only fifteen tech families, and three work with Nation Security, including mine. Psalm is the sitting botanist for the family. How she wrestled the position from her older brother only Yah knew. In addition to that it says she graduated around the time I did, so two years early. The amount of work she had to put in to be where she is now put our conversation in the garden in perspective. It makes her scolding even funnier. She is a serious person.

My thumb scrolled through her Jiacom page. All of her pictures are clean and polished. Her posts and videos come across as artificially genuine. Her friends list is very active in the comments section, eating up her videos and posts. I could smell fakeness from a mile away. It isn't malicious. It is more protective. She doesn't feel safe with people. Even though that is a lot to assume based on her social media, my gut told me that I'm not too far off. Her page is almost too perfect. Pictures featuring rows and rows of crops, videos of her making complicated concepts simple, time with her friends, and her smile in the setting sunlight.

My fingers took a screenshot. I want to embed that smile into my brain.

What am I thinking? She is just some woman back home.

The screenshot disappears in the digital trash, and I log out of Jiacom for good measure. Worrying about being marriage material has never crossed my mind. Deeping diving on a woman's social media isn't even on the playing field. She is just another woman who was seen through the lens of whiskey. My sketchbook is still empty, which should be my primary concern, not a Song Flower during Kwanzaa.

Five

Psalm

EZRI IS A GENIUS.

"Only you would think of doing this," I whisper to him.

We are deep in downtown LA, watching the sunrise in an amazing hotel.

"This way, we get to have a little more space and still meet our obligations."

Ujima, day three, is all about helping those who are less fortunate.

In the Nation, we want for nothing. We have our own schools, grocery stores, shops, and restaurants. There is even a hospital in the palace and clinics all around. We defeat the myth that Black people can't thrive or be great. It is sad that every Black person can't experience this safety and support, so we go out of our way to donate, advocate, and work toward them being as safe and secure as we are. Even if they don't live in our community, they are still our responsibility.

Azura hands me a cup of coffee and sits next to me on the balcony.

"This has been a good year," she whispers.

"Well, it's not over yet," Ezri says, sipping his iced coffee while he hands out breakfast pastries.

"Eat up because we have a lot to do today. Giveaways at shelters, food drives, and drinking, always drinking."

We laugh together. They all got ready while I focused on the cheese, egg, and beef bacon pastry. Soul's eyes flash in my mind, making blush color my cheeks. The muscles in his back flexing as he lifted the mulch was another pretty memory. I blush deeper, surprising myself. I'd only had one boyfriend before, and most of that was because Ezri said it would be criminal not to have at least one secret boyfriend in high school. He and other friends pushed two shy people together, and we just ran with it. I haven't dated since. Dating doesn't matter to me. Did it now?

"Psalm! Let's go."

I drain my coffee cup and jump into the shower. After letting my mom talk my ear off, I get dressed. No one will be where we are going. Ezri religiously checked as many social calendars as possible to give us the most privacy. While Azura and Ariyah opted for traditional abayas, I am going for something much more comfortable — long, wide, airy joggers with an oversized white t, and an abaya-style hoodie that meets the pants at my ankles. To the untrained eye, it looks like I am still wearing a dress. It is the ultimate comfort. I don't have to worry if I get caught, and the fabric feels like clouds on my skin. My white headdress and beige headphones complete the beige look.

"Risky, risky," Ariyah says.

"Let's go, guys," Ezri groans, yanking us out the door,

It is chilly on the streets. People are out in full force, getting ready for New Year's Day. Luckily for us, our new year isn't until April. It's puzzling that pagans celebrate the new year when everything is dying. It makes no sense to me, but a lot of things don't.

The minute we step out of the hotel, I have a joint in between my lips.

"You're really pushing it today." Azura laughs.

"With the way my aunties treated me at the party, I need some relief."

The smoke is comforting, and by the time we make it to the food pantry, I am better than relaxed. The director meets us at the door.

"Thank you so much for coming. The people will truly appreciate it. Most folks forget about them after the holidays."

"On the contrary, we want to thank you for giving us the space to help the community," Ezri answers.

The kitchen is already set up and ready to go. We spent all night preparing the meal of baked chicken, bone marrow mashed potatoes, and garlic green beans. We also packed them take-home care packages filled with foods they could cook on the fly, a week of free hotel stays, and gift cards for clothing. We want to have a lasting impact on their lives. We aren't just here to pass out plates.

Ezri found the blackest, poorest food kitchen he could find, just to be sure our resources were going to the correct place. It never fails to sadden me to see Black families lined up for help, but we were glad to help them. I am happy we brought toys along with us. Who knows if the children got enough presents at Christmas time. We talk with the people and pass out the bags and gifts. Ariyah brought fancy body wash sets for parents and little holiday treats.

Once we get through serving what feels like three hundred people. we mingle with the people. It makes my eyes tear up when they open the bags and see what's inside.

"Excuse me?" a woman says, tapping me on the shoulder.

"Yes."

"Are you all responsible for these bags?"

"Yes, is that eno—"

She yanks me into a hug, and I hold her while she cries.

"You don't understand. My daughter and I have three weeks until we move into housing. I didn't know where we were going to go. Shelters have been denying me left and right. We don't even have a car to sleep in. Thank you. Thank you."

I have to force her to take more hotel stays. They shouldn't have to worry about where they will sleep tonight. She is almost back on her feet, and she just needs a little more help. We move on to the next shelter and then do a drive that is only care packages.

We are on our way to our final shelter when we run into Soul and his friends. Diana pulls me into a hug right away.

"Psalm, I meant to catch you at the poetry slam. How are you?"

"This can't be the woman I saw on stage. This is the same Psalm from the garden?" Soul interrupts.

"Who else would I be?"

"Is that a joint?" he asks, ignoring me.

"Yeah, you want to hit it?"

That makes everyone burst out laughing. Soul fixes me with a look.

"I don't smoke. I am setting an example."

"Of what not to do, got it."

"You're killing me," Kenji adds around his laughter.

"We're going to go ahead to the shelter, but please keep roasting Soul. He needs it," one of his friends says.

"Looks like we're going to the same place. We will walk with you." Ariyah adds, and they walk off together, leaving me with a smirking Soul.

"I'm sorry," I blurt out.

"For what?"

"If I've been too hard on you. It's all in good fun."

He chuckles. "No, it's just surprising that the woman who scolded me for poor Hebrew doesn't even have an accent when she speaks English."

"Hebrew is the language of our God, but English is the language of our pockets."

Soul's laugh caught me off guard.

"Sounds like something my grandfather would say." He adds.

"My grandmother said it to me when I was 8. It stuck. That phrase is the main reason I'm fluent in Indonesian. It's the language of money in Bali, and I have never missed a dollar."

"You're perplexing." He quips, pausing our walk.

"Nothing like what your page projects."

"You looked me up?" I cheekily joke.

Blush darkens his cheeks and I bit back my laughter and giddiness. *He looked me up.*

"I did. After I left the garden… I wanted to see who you are."

"Did you find what you were looking for?"

"I think I did now."

We share a glance and continue walking to the shelter in silence.

"What are you listening to?" he asks, wiggling my headphones.

"My favorite album. It sounds better on my record player."

"Let me guess. Is it Micheal Tumbo or Michelle Agave?"

"No, not a Nation artist. It's Stevie Wonder."

"*Songs in the Key of Life?*"

He laughs at the surprise on my face.

"You seem like that type, but a record player? Does that also mean vinyl collection? I bet you don't have the classics."

"Try me?"

"*Ben?*" he quizzes.

"Pft, of course. Michael Jackson is the shit. He is one of my favorites. I have the original *Thriller* vinyl as well."

"What about Anita Baker?"

"From *Rapture* to *The Best of Anita.*"

"Okay, this is a hard one, George Bridgewater?"

"As soon as they pressed it," I answered.

He chuckles again, and we stand at the steps of the shelter. The smoke creates a delicate screen between us.

"She smokes, curses, listens to pagan music, and speaks perfect Hebrew. Who are you, Song Flower?" he whispers.

"Wouldn't you like to know?" My voice is breathless.

"Psalm, come on. This is our last stop," Azura interrupts us, yanking me inside.

Soul's eyes never leave me as the door closes behind us.

Soul

We have one more stop to make after we leave the shelter where Psalm is. It is hard for me to focus after that. The two images of her in my mind make her Jiacom make more sense. The woman smoking with one headphone on her ear is the real Psalm. She is in street clothes, a hoodie, and sweatpants. Although modest, she looks *cool*. It makes me feel childish to reveal that to myself, but that is all I could think of when we approached her. She knows about little-known Black composers and about how good Michael Jackson's early albums are. She is feisty and beautiful. All of that means I should keep my distance. How do I keep my distance?

Tree is right. My friends know me well. The more I learn about Psalm, the more I know she should be left alone. My life isn't in LA. My life is in New York, and it will stay that way for the foreseeable future. The community is big, and the activities are plentiful. Psalm and I should be able to stay away from each other. If we make it through Kwanzaa then we will never have to see each other again. We can become a distant holiday memory. An ache spreads through my heart as I think the words. No matter what I feel a memory would have to be enough.

We go back to my place and hang out in the backyard for the rest of the night. Tade and Isra joined us underneath the stars.

"So Isra, did you know Soul is in love?" Diana starts.

Tree spit out his tea, and Tade laughs out loud.

"Yah himself will come back before he falls in love," Isra says.

"It's true," Xaevi adds.

"Her name is Psalm."

"Rose?" Tade exclaims.

"How do you know her?" I ask.

"Not personally. She is big on Jiacom because of the different causes she supports. A lot of my friends follow her. She's for sure a good girl. I thought that wasn't your type."

"It's not."

"Then why do you blush every time someone says her name?"

"I don't!"

"Well, they took their sweet time walking into the shelter today. She practically had to be dragged away from him."

"Diana, stop talking," I exclaim, but it is too late. Isra is already glaring at me.

"Soul, I told you to stay away from her."

Isra is starting to make me angry.

"Do you really think I am such a terrible man? I'm your brother. You know me."

"Of course, I don't think you're terrible. I just think you are indecisive. There is no point in either one of you getting hurt. Deep down, you're a lover boy. You want to be loved romantically, but you're scared, so you play with pagan women because you know there isn't an inkling you'll take them seriously. This isn't New York, and Psalm is not pagan. There is more at risk here."

"Don't you think I know that? Plus, this is all hypothetical. I think she is cool, but I don't have feelings for her like that."

"You were always bad at lying," Tree whispers.

"How about we have some s'mores? Tomorrow is Village Day!" Diana says, trying to change the subject.

"Oh yeah! The best day of Kwanzaa!" Tade cheers.

"I heard everyone is pulling out the stops this year — new recipes from the restaurants, unreleased clothing from the shops, and new artists dropping some fly pieces. It's going to be the best one yet," Xaevi says, dancing.

"Soul, are you selling this year?" Kenji asks.

"No," I angrily reply.

I have not let Isra's comments go, and I leave them at the bonfire. Isra follows me.

"Soul, wait up!"

"Leave me alone, Isra."

"Just hear me out, please."

"You've said enough."

She yanks me to a halt by my arm.

"Do you remember when we were in high school, and you had a crush on Penelope Benson?"

"Yeah, what's your point?"

"You asked her to prom, but when you got to her house, she had already left with another boy. You didn't come out of your room for a week."

"Again, what's your point?"

"This time, it won't be another boy. It'll be life that pushes you and Psalm apart. I don't know what your week in the room would be now. I just want you to be okay. If you were home and had taken over the business, I wouldn't say anything, but you're still exploring right now. When you drop your anchor while you're still moving, it could bring the entire ship down."

"It won't."

"You don't know that."

"Neither do you."

"Soul, did Zaraki give you the tunic I picked out?"

The heavy dress bag in my hand swung in mom's direction, and she nodded, continuing her tirade. Ujamaa is all about money, baby. Day Four is about keeping the black dollar in the Black community. Everyone spends the most money during this time. Sometimes, they keep what they buy, but they usually send the things they purchase as gifts for family and friends who couldn't make it or donations towards people who could use the items. Even the royal family dumps buckets of money into the village. All the money we spend in the village gets sent to different causes — helping people of color buy houses and escape redlining, spending money on transportation so people can make it to their jobs, and whatever other cause we can get behind.

My mom is becoming increasingly insufferable, so I take a walk. People are locking up their shops and setting up lavish booths. The smell of baked goods is already in the air. Men and women are hanging up lavish abayas and tunics on their hooks. There were already a few I had my eye on. A blood orange and gold abaya caught my eye. Psalm would look amazing in it. It would make her eyes pop. Reluctantly, my body made me gravitate toward the half-built booth.

"If it isn't Soul." Mrs. Baker chuckles.

"How are you, Mrs. Baker?"

"Great, of course, the mister could be doing better, but Yah makes no mistakes."

"That he doesn't.."

She caught me staring at the abaya.

"See something you like?" she quizzes.

"Yes, how much?"

"You know we can't start selling until things get started."

"I know, but could you make an exception for me? Just this once."

"Fine, but you owe me a favor."

"Gladly."

She packed the abaya and head wrap in a decorative black box and then in a gold bag. All the presents for my friends and family were purchased ahead of time, each one fitting the theme of the day, but this is the first time I have ever brought a gift for someone I don't know. It was fun watching them open gifts each day. Sometimes, they think I don't think about them, but that couldn't be further from the truth. On top of that, clothes are personal gifts, and men never give unmarried women clothes. I can't even give this to Psalm in front of others. It's a stupid idea. I just...want to see the color on her glowing skin. She would wear it so well. Hopefully, this is her size. She tends to wear her clothes looser than others. It is the first thing I noticed about her. There is so much to notice.

Now that my head is clear, Isra's comments have shifted perspective. My heart is delicate, and the best way to protect myself is never to put down roots. It is the safest way to move. Psalm would be more than putting down roots. Isra is right about the risk. My choices wouldn't just affect me, but Psalm too. Even giving her this dress could make other families shy away from courting her. Still, Isra could have had this conversation with me privately.

When my mom started blowing up my phone, I knew it was time to go back. My sketchbook caught my eye before my shower. This lack of inspiration is getting more and more frustrating. We can't even decide on a venue until the theme comes together. Nothing is coming to mind. Usually, ideas flow at the end of each show, but there is no direction this time. It is like having a stuffy nose. You know you can breathe, and you miss being able to. Without creativity, there is no art, which leaves me disconnected from my purpose. It is almost like being naked.

"Hey, are you okay?" Tade asks, leaning against the door frame.

"Yeah, why wouldn't I be?"

"Isra was a little hard on you."

"Well, she always has been."

Tade fastens the button on my brown cashmere tunic for me.

"This is going to be controversial but cut Isra some slack."

"Please go on."

He fastens my chocolate diamond watch as he continues. "She's just trying to protect you. Being the oldest doesn't make you exempt from that."

"It didn't feel like protecting. It feels like she doesn't believe in me. Like she thinks I'm a bad person."

"If that is the message you got, then I'm sorry, Soul," Isra apologized, standing at the doorway.

"Let me go help, Mom." Tade excused himself.

"Maybe we could have discussed it in private, but you don't understand what it's like being a woman in the Nation. Anything can ruin your reputation. Hell, if you're unmarried and you talk to a man for too long, you may be implicated. Psalm is on the marriage market, and her family takes it very seriously."

On the market?

Isra looked like she didn't want to tell me that, but it's not like it matters.

"You're right, but I'm telling you that it is not lost on me. My intentions are pure."

"I know. Maybe I'm scared too."

"Well, let's be scared together," I answer, offering my hand.

Damn, the people showed *up* for Village Day. There are so many different colors, sights, and sounds. To make it even worse, it is cold for California right now. That didn't stop anyone from coming out, and it looks like everyone is going to have fun.

"Soul, are you going to win me a stuffed animal?," my youngest sister Olaya asks

"Of course. It wouldn't be Village Day if I didn't."

She pulls me into a hug, and we start as a family. For some reason, Psalm's present is tucked into the bag, and in my hand no one questions it. They more than likely assumed it was for Diana. If I found Psalm, she would get it, but if I didn't see her tonight, then the abaya would get donated. That felt like a good line to draw. Boundaries.

It doesn't take me long to win Olaya her stuffed animal or to beat Dad in a shooting arcade game. Everyone kind of goes off on their own after a few hours. The night is waxing late, and I am sure Psalm won't see me. Suddenly there she was. Her back at the hot cider stand. The brown abaya she wore glimmered in the light. When she laughs, my feet carry me to the booth.

Psalm

"Psalm," Soul calls.

Before I turn around, I know it's him. The poetry slam has cemented his voice in my mind, and it's hard not to smile.

"Soul, how are you enjoying Village Day?"

"Better now."

He looks surprised that he said that.

"Anyway, how is the cider?"

"It was better last year when the Timbe's made it," I whisper, and he laughs out loud.

It's a beautiful laugh.

"The hand pies were better last year, too."

We fall in step together, and it's nice. There isn't a need for conversation. It's just vibes. Silence with Soul is comfortable.

"It's surprising you don't have headphones in."

"They couldn't be hidden under my head wrap."

We share more laughter, careful to keep our distance, which is difficult. It's like being in orbit.

"Village Day is my favorite day, though. I wouldn't miss this for anything in the world. It's like all of us are breathing as one organism."

Rambling is a famous trait of mine. I turn to Soul, embarrassed, but he's listening *genuinely*.

"If you could be doing anything else right now, what would it be?"

"There is this soil composition they use on farms in South Africa. I think it could do wonders for us. I didn't get to test the samples before I left."

"You don't have to do that."

"Do what?" I ask, confused.

"Tell me what you think I want to hear. Give me a real answer."

That answer was the perfect amount of truth and a lie. I do want to test those samples, but not in place of this moment.

"Well, there is this doll I've been working on for a long time now," I admit vulnerably.

Ugh, that was way too personal.

"Dolls?"

"It started as a therapy project, then I started making them for all the girls who want to see themselves as pretty."

"And this doll?"

"It's for Little Psalm," I squeak out.

Why was all this personal information spilling out of me? The questions he asked, I had rehearsed answers for. If one answer doesn't land you try another. You never spill your secrets. Why am I letting him in?

"That's a good idea. Maybe I should make a guitar for Little Soul."

"You make instruments?" Surprise colors my voice.

"Oh yeah, it feels nice to do something that doesn't get much recognition."

"You don't like being known as the genius next to run the giant?"

"No." He answers curtly.

If I am bearing my truths, so would he.

"Why?"

"It's…difficult imagining the responsibility. It's why I ended up doing art in New York in the first place."

"You ran?"

"I went to find myself. I'm still looking." He chuckles at the end but looks broken.

"Do you like being known for your art?"

"Yes, but when people know you for something or know you're good at something, they expect more from you. The people who know I make guitars and pianos don't care about my name, just the instruments."

"Sounds nice, getting to disappear into something," I offered since he was being so transparent.

"You could've disappeared and let your older brother run things. Why did you choose to take over?"

Psalm, use the press answer. Use the press answer.

"Jazz didn't want to take over. He prefers architecture but knows our mom wouldn't let it go if he walked away. So I fought like hell for it. Believe me, it was quite a fight. Plus, it's natural for me. Mother Nature chose me for this, so I took it."

"What's your favorite part?"

"Solving the earth's problems by sampling the soil. It tells you all the secrets to fixing things. We are trying to create something that can protect the soil and the plant it sprouts from pollutants but it's been difficult. If we do that, it would be easier to fix problems."

I lingered by a booth. "Sorry, I am rambling."

"Don't be sorry for your passion. It sounds like a life-changing project."

"It could be. We could prevent the soil absorbing pesticides, microplastics, or anything else that can be harmful"

He got excited. "You know my family is in tech. You should look into using nanos to help you with the project. I am sure someone could make it. If not, I can."

Soul is known for not running his family business and doing

art instead. People lambast him for it, but to me, it's brave. He chose to chase his passions. Few people get the option to do that.

"Sounds like someone likes the family business."

"I always have. I just like art more."

We stop on the edge of the market, and I take a step in his direction. This is dangerous.

"Oh, this is for you. My apologies if it is too personal. I just... thought you would like it."

He hands me the bag. It perplexes me. Soul doesn't know me, so what could be inside?

"Psalm, there you are," Novali's voice broke through the crowd.

We took a step apart before she approached us. Her eyes dart to Soul but don't linger.

"Mom wants us to take a family picture. You know the snow is going to melt soon," she excitedly says.

I clutch the bag as we walk through the crowd. Soul thought of me when he wasn't around. He sees through my practiced lies. That is... comforting. No, that isn't the word. It's on the tip of my tongue. I couldn't place it. Novali stops me and applies more lip gloss. The realization that she had lied crosses my mind as she snatches the bag out of my hand and pushes me forward. Mom is standing next to a gorgeous woman her age. In between the woman and the man is a guy my age. His long, thick locs framed his strong jawline and gentle gaze. *Oh no.*

"Psalm, this is the Idrissi family."

I shake the mother's hand and place my hand over my heart for the father. The guy turns to me.

"My name is Joa."

"He is going to be your future husband," Mom excitedly announces.

My smile stays, and I offer him my hand over my heart.

"It will be wonderful to get to know you, Psalm."

"I could say the same for you."

Thankfully, our parents do all the talking, and Novali pulls me back by her side. We are lucky Chyna is off with Abraham's family. Jazz and Chanson share looks all night. At one point, they caught a glare from my mother, so we all found this out together.

The Idrissi's are nice, and his mom is pleasant, but I can't stop thinking about Soul's laughter. Plus, there is no way I am going to be able to stay in Bali. Mom and I would fight, and then this would blow over. There are only three more days left in Kwanzaa. It wouldn't be hard to last that long. Right?

Novali could have warned me before. Faking it would have been easier, but she let Mom blindside me. Mom wouldn't let me out of sight the rest of the night. She keeps me close while talking up my accolades. Joa and I keep sharing looks. He is cute, of course, but we don't know each other. Mom doesn't even know if we are compatible. This all feels too soon. I shouldn't have agreed to this.

———

The moment we are home, I turn on my sister.

"You could have at least given me a heads up."

"Mom didn't want me to."

"Since when do you let her come between us?"

"I didn't."

"Novali, you let me walk right into the lion's den."

She bit her lip. "I didn't think you would come if you knew."

"You didn't even give me a chance." I sigh, defeated.

The cool air from the balcony reminds me of the plants outside. Carefully, I pluck the bud from the plant and roll a joint. The muscle memory calms me. Novali sits beside me and says nothing.

"You always keep your composure. I trusted that."

The sound of the lighter and the sizzle of the herb calms me further.

"Barely. You don't know what I go through to keep up that face."

My honesty from my conversation with Soul wouldn't serve me here. Novali wouldn't get it. She only gets half of me.

"You're my big sister. You are supposed to help me navigate this, and you failed me tonight."

"It's not easy standing between you and Mom. Give me a break, Psalm."

"Don't I always? This is the only time I expected you to pick me."

She gives me the gold bag, and my attention immediately shifts. Novali watches as the decorative black box slides out of the bag. Inside is a gorgeous blood-orange abaya. It's made of a material that is foreign to me, but it's light and airy — a summer abaya. The blush that colors my cheeks is full and deep. He isn't supposed to buy me clothes. It's nearly forbidden.

"Where did you get that?" she inquires.

It's my turn to lie to her.

"Ariyah gave it to me. She brought it back from Morocco."

"It's totally your color."

"And my size," I whisper.

It is one size up from the abayas my mother bought me, which I prefer. He picked up on that too.

"So, what did I miss? That abaya is amazing," Chyna notes, plucking the joint from my fingers.

"How was the village?" Novali gently asks.

"It was fun. Abraham won me an elephant. Anything exciting happens with you guys?"

And the floodgates will open in 3..2..1

"Psalm met her future husband today."

Chyna's head whips in my direction.

"Psalm... how do you feel right now?"

"I'm freaking the fuck out. Joa looks nice, but we don't even know each other. I have never even heard of him. On top of that, he doesn't even have a Jiacom page. *Everyone* has a page."

"Mom put together a profile for you," Novali offers.

Chyna tosses it into the empty chair.

"That's only going to tell her what the family wants her to know."

"It's better than nothing, which is what she has now," Novali asserts.

"Psalm, you don't have to do any of this. It is well within your rights to walk down to Mom's office and tell her no."

"Chyna, we don't even know how this is going to turn out," Novali argues.

"Can you guys just leave, please?" My quiet voice broke through their debate.

"Psalm," Chyna says sadly.

"Please."

They share a glance before walking back into my room. The tears didn't come until I heard my room door close.

Panic rises in my chest. Joa could be nice, but he could be cruel. He could be everything I ever wanted, or he could be my worst nightmare, but the thing is, I don't want anything. If it were up to me, there wouldn't be a marriage, but everything isn't about me all the time. That is why I agreed in the first place. I owe my family the continuation of this bloodline. I owe my community more members. Joa seems like a gentle, kind man. This could work. The breeze blew the scent of the abaya my way.

"Please," I scoff aloud, rolling my eyes.

Soul is handsome and gentle. There is hope that he really likes me. Maybe that is where my heart is leaning and I am fighting it. He is flighty and unpredictable. At least, that is what I hear. In fact, before this, he was a vague memory from a different high school. They posted him on Jiacom when he graduated early and started working for his dad's company. That was the last time any of us heard of him until he left for New York. It is always news when one of us leaves home.

Mom would find some way to say no, anyway. Deep down that bothers me.

Surprisingly, she is giving me space. Chyna and Novali are the angel and demon on my shoulders that you usually see in cartoons. I just don't know which is the angel and the demon. Chyna is still naive, and Novali is too complacent. Where is the middle ground? Could I be that middle ground with Joa?

The wind blew the sheets of his profile my way, catching in my hand before they could slip off the balcony. He looks cute in his profile picture. The smile on his face is natural. He is a marine biologist. He works in Bali and is a chef in his spare time. The pictures of him in the water are the most relaxed. The water is his happy place like the trees are mine. It's cute. Of course, he wants children. He also doesn't want to leave Bali and move back to LA. I am probably the only Nation woman in the world he would marry. Joa has two dogs and moved out of his parents' house for the ocean. He is a free spirit like me in a lot of ways. Still, this is on paper. Joa could be a completely different person when we got to talking.

I put the joint out and grabbed the throw off the back of the couch. My body stretched and relaxed into the cushions. We would try both of their advice. Joa deserves to at least get to prove his character, but I won't stop being cautious.

Six

THE SMELL of chamomile tea delicately pulls me out of sleep.

"Good morning, princess," my dad whispers.

He looks softly at the rising sun. My head is foggy as I sit up, eyes squinting in the sunlight. The tea warms my bones. Sleeping outside was a bad idea.

"How are you this morning?" he questions.

"Better than yesterday, so you like the Idrissi's?"

"They are a nice family. They have also been working on new irrigation technology. It's cutting edge."

Ah, I see.

"Hmm, what about them, though?"

"Well, they aren't involved in rumors, make a decent amount of money, and are genuinely looking to get to know you, so they are off to a good start."

His brow furrows, indicating that he is serious.

"You don't have to ever see them again if you don't want to."

"It's okay. We should at least give them a chance, especially if they have your pre-approval."

"Once you're done with your tea, get dressed. Mom needs you and Jazz to pick up the flowers and check in with the caterer."

"I literally just opened my eyes."

"Yeah, well, the house woke up hours ago."

Having my dad's support took some of the fear out of it. Maybe this could work out.

Jazz was waiting for me at the bottom of the stairs. "We're going to be late because of you."

"Hold your damn horses. Looking this good takes time."

"Boo, bad joke," Chanson chants as we walk out of the door.

"So, a lot happened last night."

"Jazz, let's just enjoy the day."

"I haven't heard any bad things about him."

"Have you heard good things?"

"Well, what I have heard is that Joa is a quiet dude who doesn't bother anyone."

"Which is code for he doesn't let people close enough to know much about him."

"You're such a cynic."

"No, I'm making an observation."

"Potato, potato." He shrugs.

"All I'm saying is that. When Mom gave me Sherie's profile, I didn't read it. All of that stuff could be made up for all I know. You can't fake reality. It is harder to keep up appearances in person, so my focus was on the dates. Sherie's real personality is almost nothing like her profile."

Jazz got close to my ear.

"Plus, you know I would murder him if he even thought about hurting you."

I push him away, and he laughs us into the parking lot.

It seems Mom ordered all the flowers in the damn shop because the entire truck was filled when we drove back. I ended up sneezing all the way back home.

Mom gives me a cup of Butterbur tea as soon as we enter the door.

"Chyna should've gone instead. I always forget about your flower allergy until the last minute."

"Thank you. I'll take this to my room."

I left no room for her protest and went up to my room, quickly went up the ladder, and waited. As expected, Mom walked out on the balcony minutes later.

"Where the hell did that girl go?"

Once, I am sure she is gone. I spark up and drink the tea. Mom always shows she cares when you think she doesn't. It is almost like having whiplash sometimes. Or maybe I still see her the way a child sees a parent as just a parent. She knows pressures I don't know about yet.

I sit up here for as long as I can. Mom found her way back into the room as soon as I was back inside.

"Alright, it is fundraiser night. Joa and his family are coming. It will be the perfect night for you to get to know him." She cheerfully grabs a dress bag. "And you are going to be a vision in your great-grandmother's dress."

"Mom, I don't know if I can do this. We are moving too fast."

"We are not. This is the perfect place for us to be, baby."

"I don't know if I want to marry Joa."

"You are thinking too far ahead. Let's focus on this party."

She pauses, waiting for me to protest further, but it just isn't in me tonight. Chyna and Novali's fighting has taken the wind out of my sails. I just want to get this night over with so I can relax and put my feet up.

"I can get myself dressed."

The whisper interrupted my mom's cheery deposition.

"Psalm..."

"Not tonight, Mom. Just let me get dressed, please."

She left, and I got myself into the luxury abaya. The dress is gorgeous. Each layer of the tulle is a vibrant red, with the last layer being yellow. The red organza is one-shouldered with a vibrant yellow silk shirt underneath. It is a royal look. For some reason, that brings tears to my eyes. This dress would have all eyes on me. I get that tonight is all about being dazzling when it should have been about purpose. That is what Nia is all about. Our purpose is to do everything we can to help other Black people live full lives. So, all across the Nation, fundraisers are going on left and right.

Our fundraiser is very special because all the money collected is going toward rebuilding some of the worst living quarters in California. Consistently, people of color have been left to rot in crumbling housing projects. They deserve a lot better than they are getting, so people put on their best and brightest, show up, and donate hundreds of thousands of dollars.

"Hey, your mom forgot your head wrap," Sherie says, waltzing in.

It totally slips my mind that my bun is uncovered.

"Thank you."

"Any time, baby sister." She chuckles, slipping the wrap into place.

Since the day the engagement was announced, Sherie has gotten close with all of us. She affectionately calls me her little sister because she has never had one. She and Novali are the same age, which is more like gaining a peer.

"Forgive me, but Jazz said you are nervous about this whole thing."

"I'm a wreck, to be exact."

"I was too. When my mother brought me Jazz's profile, he was so handsome, but it was scary. When we get married, we leave our families and move into new homes. That means new customs, traditions, and rules."

"How did you get over it?"

"Well, I had you and Novali. Your parents are also lovely. We all hear nightmare stories about mothers-in-law, but I am very blessed."

Sherie drops the ruby and yellow diamond headpiece on my head.

"My family also has my back, and I know your family will have yours. Trust them." Sherie squeezed my hand and went to get my nephew dressed.

The fundraiser is due to start in an hour. Mom has invited everyone she knows and they are coming out. Even families on the fringes are coming. The house would be so filled that we have to open the backyard and surrounding land. They spent the entire day decorating and making sure paths were illuminated properly.

Novali walks into my room with my lip gloss in hand.

"Would you stop taking my stuff?" I groan, snatching the lip gloss from her. It perfectly completes my look.

"Did you see the pictures Davi posted on Jiacom? He's really trying to pass this pagan off as Nation royalty. It's disgusting."

She tosses me her phone, and there is Mikiea, dazzling but still looking out of place. In the video, she is still struggling to walk in her abayas. What makes it worse is that on Kira's page, she is gliding down the stairs in an elegant fashion. She is perfect.

"That's what happens when privilege gets to you," I comment, tossing the phone back to her.

Novali continues shit-talking the royal family's newest member as we head down the stairs to take another one of Mom's family pictures. To my surprise, the rest of the family is in white. I am the only one in red. Another point in Mom's plan, no doubt. In the past, I would care less, but my heart almost can't stand whatever she was planning.

As soon as it hits seven o'clock, people are walking through the door. Perfume and soft scents filled the house, and Mom stuck Chyna and me with greeting them. It's fun, though. We get a chance to chat briefly with people we haven't seen in years. Chyna and I are having a good time until the Idrissi's approach me.

"We are so glad you could make it," I comment while shaking his mom's hand.

"It's wonderful to be here. Your mother was telling me about the gardens outback. Would you mind giving me a tour?" Joa asks.

"Of course. I'll be happy to show you my favorite parts."

As soon as I step away, Novali slides into my place. Mom is always prepared and sees us from across the room. We don't need a chaperone since there are eyes everywhere. The air gives me a break from the stifling heat that has built up inside.

"So, are you just as nervous about this as I am?" he bashfully asks.

"Absolutely, it's... new for me."

"Me too."

"Why do you want to get married?" I blurt.

He smirked. "For one, it's about time. My parents want grandchildren, and my brother isn't as responsible as he should be. For two, I want to fall in love, but few Nation women want to live in Bali. It isn't as glamorous as the Nation's capital. This is the help I need."

Joa stops us underneath the birch tree brimming with lights. Under the tree, his hazel eyes are gentle.

"Psalm, I know this is sudden, but I want us to get to know each other. This should be both of our choices. Ask me anything you want to know."

"Why marine biology?"

"It's important to me that no matter what we have our hands in, we make sure we aren't damaging those ecosystems for our own gains. The pagans do it enough for all of us."

That piqued my interest. Joa takes me around the rose bushes as we toss ideas back and forth. He cracks jokes most of the time, which takes a lot of pressure off me. He is *nice,* so why am I still skeptical?

Soul

Psalm's home is expansive, taking in the property inspires a low whistle. Who knew our moms went to college together and stayed in touch? She was the first one on the invite list for this fundraiser, which means we all would get dragged along with her. I was going to find some reason not to go until she told me the last name of the family. There is only one Rose family in the Nation. Nothing was going to stop me from being at this party. In the distance, my sister comes into view. Isra and her husband are in rare form tonight. When she is with him, it is like she is a different person. Isra isn't bossy, loud, or imposing. She is just Isra. It is a pleasant break. Mom starts introducing Tade to all the available families, so it's just me, especially since Dad is off somewhere with Psalm's father.

The whiskey in my glass gradually disappears as I search for her. My top worry is that she is upset about the abaya. It came from an innocent place but could be interpreted as making a pass at her. I hope she isn't too upset with me, but in order for me to confirm that I have to find her. The place is packed, with the crowd confined to the first floor. The party spills out into the backyard, which is dazzling and well-designed.

Before my eyes could find Psalm, Dad found me.

"Soul, are you enjoying the party?"

"It's really nice. We should throw something like this."

"Do me a favor and don't say that to your mother." He laughs.

"Dad, when did you know you were ready for marriage?"

"When I met your mother. She walked up to me at a party and told me my mother raised me better than I was acting." He laughs again.

"I went to my father the next morning and told him I found my wife. We got married six months later and never looked back."

"What's the best part of marriage?"

"How much your mother loves me. We weren't always in the position we are today. My father lost the royal contract, and we had to let go of half our employees. It felt like I had failed. Your mother kissed me on the forehead, connected me with the right people, and never let my head fall again. She's amazing, still beautiful, funny, and intelligent. There is nothing I was more sure about than your mother."

He grew serious.

"Son, you and your art could benefit from having the right woman at your side, and I am willing to let up pressure about you taking over if you settle down with someone. It'll get your mom off your back, too."

"I'll consider it. I admit being home this time feels different. There is so much I thought I knew about this place. I don't know anything."

"That's not giving yourself enough credit. You know a lot of things, just not what you're looking to know now. Whatever that is. When you are ready, I will help you figure things out."

He heads to where my mother is standing. Suddenly, a scent drifts to me on the breeze, causing me to look around covertly. There is Psalm. She is absolutely stunning in that red gown. The jewels on her headpiece can't even outshine her. The crowd gently parts as I walk in her direction. Someone else moves, and a man comes into view. Psalm tosses her head back in laughter, stopping me in my tracks. Then he touches her arm.

Oh, he must be...

"Her mom announced it to her friends at the village yesterday, but nothing is set in stone," Isra says behind me.

"I thought you were on a leash tonight."

"I'm going to let that one slide since you've been drinking."

"It's not like I really care, anyway."

"You can keep lying to yourself all you want, Soul, but you know you feel something for her. You wouldn't have bought her an abaya if you didn't."

She smirks at me. "Don't ask how I know. If you want Psalm, you will have to show her family you're a better pick than Joa."

"I don't want her."

"If you say so," she sings before leaving me with my thoughts.

The lights on the trail guide me away from the rest of the party to the quiet of the trees behind the home. I sit on the bench someone made out of a dead tree. The twinkling path is my only guide back.

Isra and Tree saw through my lies no matter how hard I try. Above all else, lying to myself is the easiest thing for me to do. The truth is always harder. If I am being honest with myself. I feel in love with her. The thought causes me to exhale and drop my head into my hands.

How could I not? Psalm is beautiful, intelligent, passionate, and hilarious. I could picture myself living in Bali six months out of the year. Visualizing her sitting on my kitchen counter with a mug in her hand back in New York felt natural. Maybe she would let me teach her how to sculpt. I could learn how she makes her dolls. We could watch the ball drop on pagan New Year or go ice skating. She would love it in New York. Sleep would escape me every night because I would stay up late, watching her breathe in and out.

I have never been in love before. The feeling is all-consuming to the point where it takes my breath away. He doesn't deserve to touch her arm or listen to her talk about her passions. It should be me watching her chase her dreams. Psalm is supposed to be mine. That thought led me to question myself. Did I truly want her?

Psalm isn't like any other Nation woman I know. She is vibrant and alive. Psalm is authentically herself in person, and it's refreshing. Would the novelty of her vibrancy wear off? Am I so infatuated because she is new to me? There is so much to consider outside of my feelings, but none of that matters when she looks at me. She even turned and smiled when she heard me call her name. She knew it was me. Psalm isn't afraid to poke fun at me or apologize when she feels like she is wrong. My heart aches just thinking about her laughter. I want it all for myself, and I want to spend the rest of my days making her laugh and wiping her tears.

Do I tell her? Was this something she would want to know? Does she even feel the same way about me?

I don't want to complicate her life, force myself on her, or assume that she has the same feelings as me. The smooth wood is cool on my back as I lay down to take in the treetops. If I am truly falling in love with Psalm, could I give her all the things she wants out of life? What does she even want?

"Romeo, Romeo. Wherefore art thou Romeo," Tree laughingly calls.

"Call me but love, and I'll be new baptized," I whisper.

"Oh, I haven't seen emo Soul since high school. Tell me what's troubling you," he inquires, putting my legs in his lap as he sits down.

"Only if you promise not to tell Diana."

"You have my word."

"Tree... I think I love her."

"Diana! That's gross, and she's spoken for," he exclaims.

"No, you dunce. Psalm. I think I am in love with her," I answer, sitting up and shoving him.

"What do you want to do about it?"

"I don't know. My primary concern is making sure she doesn't get hurt. She deserves the best life has to offer."

"You're a good dude, Soul. I know you could give her the world."

"What if this is just me being infatuated with her, and then I pursue, and a year from now, all those emotions are gone? She deserves better than a brooding, indecisive artist."

"If that's all you think you are, then you may be right. Psalm doesn't deserve that Soul. She deserves the one who fought for Diana's honor, the Soul that flew to London during Kenji's quarter-life crisis, or the Soul that makes sure he catches all of Xaevi's Olympic events or never forgets his mom's birthday. You are such a loving, kind, and caring man. You deserve to be all of yourself, and you deserve to be loved." Tree slapped me on my back before dragging me back to the party.

I watched Psalm the entire night, hoping she would let the facade slip and I would see that she didn't want him, but she never broke, or she really likes him. It's hard for me to tell. That hurts, but if this guy is good for her, could make her happy, and if she wants him, who am I to interfere? Who knows if I could be any of that for her?

Finally, my mom gathers us to go, and for the first time that night, Psalm catches my gaze. She is finally away from Joa and looks like she wants to come over to me. Once she angles her body toward my direction, my body does the same, but someone grabs her arm and pulls her back inside. She tries to pull away, but they say something, and she ends up following them, looking back at me all the while. There is guilt in her soft features. Her eyes shine with it, but she doesn't owe me guilt. She doesn't owe me anything. It's a mystery that she would feel that she does.

"Tonight is so great," Mom drunkenly sings as we pile into the car.

Too bad we don't feel the same way.

Our voices climb over the music as we sing along to holiday jams. It is hard to keep my energy up, but that is the only way to keep them off my back. I am still processing my feelings, trying to decide what choice I should make. As I ponder, an alert from Jiacom catches my attention. Psalm's post is captioned *Songs in the Keys of Life*. There is a picture of moon-filled water. I know that beach. It's not too far from her house, and judging by the position of the moon her location isn't on the common beach. With that caption, this post feels like it's for me. Once we get home, It doesn't take me long to put on my powder blue sweater tunic and slacks.

My palms are sweating as I turn the wheel into the beach parking lot. What if I am wrong, and I show up in her private oasis? My heart tells me to get out of the car. I'm not wrong. This is her calling out for me. The moon is more beautiful in person. Its glow bathes the beach in its ethereal light. The cool grains of sand massage my feet as I start walking to where Psalm is. Jagged rigid rock on the hillside catches the moonlight. Behind a difficult path is a sliver of sand and a swell of waves.

There she is. I want to turn around. She looks too peaceful to disturb. The earlier extravagance of her gown is gone. Here she is her raw self. The light blue abaya is bathed white in the moon's shine. There is a hint of her laid hair under the loose headwrap. Psalm's skirts grace the sand. She looks like a princess, too beautiful to be from earth. Her eyes catch mine and she reaches her hand out to me, compelling me forward.

Once our hands are together she pulls me forward, our lips gently meeting. My heart explodes with this feeling. It's deeper than love. I kiss her again and again. Until Psalms's giggle brings us up for air.

"I have been wanting to do that since I fell in your lap."

Those words quieted all the questions in my head. She wants me. Psalm has always wanted me.

"About tonight, I'm sorry. My mom has her plans."

"Do you want to go along with them?" I ask.

"I don't know. Soul, I'm scared."

"Me too," I admit.

We pull each other close. Our warmth creates a cocoon. I don't know what I'm doing. Psalm is the perfect woman for me. She is everything I could want in a partner, but she comes from an old family. A founding family. They would accept nothing less than a responsible man who could provide everything for their daughter. Am I ready to be that man? Is love worth it?

"If this is the last time-"

"Hey, don't talk like that."

"I don't know if I'll see you again after Kwanzaa is over." She cries.

I wipe away her tears with my thumb.

"We don't have to worry about the future right now. Psalm, I will follow your lead. Do whatever you wish. It's your heart. Just know that I would be more than happy to hold it."

We spend a few more hours holding each other in the sand before I watch her walk home.

Seven

THIS WEEK IS FLYING BY. When I first arrived in LA, I couldn't wait to go back to New York, but now, I'd move everything back here for the chance to see Psalm every day. It is clear we want each other but are we willing to truly do what it takes? Can I give up New York? Dad and I never discussed what my coming home would look like. It seems like a stupid obstacle, but my heart is pushing me to take a chance on love. It doesn't matter if we ever cross paths again. I just want to be in the same city as her. I am sick with it. That makes me chuckle. Isra would die if she heard me say that out loud.

Mom opens the door and waltzes into my room.

"Mom, you have to knock first. What if I'm naked in here?"

"Soul, who cares? I changed your diapers. Apparently, we are doing community clean-ups today, so find something not so flashy to wear."

"I'm not sure I own anything clean-up worthy."

"Find something anyway," she says, then takes a seat on my bed.

Mom surprises me by taking my face in her hands.

"Honey, are you sure that everything is okay? You are always under so much stress during the holiday season."

"This has been the best Kwanzaa yet, Mom. I'm okay."

She gives me a concerning look that Isra had inherited.

"No, that's not why. I just miss you guys so much. Being away gets lonely."

"You know you are always welcome to come home. This suite will be waiting for you."

She gets up to leave when I blurt, "How did you know you wanted to marry Dad?"

"Well, I wasn't very soft. Being the oldest, with no brothers, I had a lot on my shoulders, but he took it all on the chin and let me be my authentic self, and every day, he still lets me be me."

"What if he would've run from you?"

"Then I wouldn't have spent one more day thinking about him. Whoever is meant for you is meant for you, and nothing is going to keep them away from you."

She kisses my forehead and starts yelling for Tade as she leaves the room.

That poses the question: Am I truly ready for that kind of love? Dad said things weren't easy. There were trials and tribulations. My parents live real lives. Am I ready to grow up for Psalm? Shouldn't this be for me?

"Everybody get a move on. We have to get to our assigned neighborhood in three hours," Dad yells up the stairs.

I take my time in the shower before being the first one dressed. Dad is happy to see me.

"Son, go get us set up. This is where the email says we should be."

Without protest, I drive over to the check-in station, and it is nearly pandemonium when I park the car. Psalm is at the head of it all, and she is barking orders left and right. Stress is painted all over her face, and I think she could be near tears.

Without thinking, I lightly jog over to her. People are asking a million questions, and she is clearly overwhelmed. So many people are talking to her that I know she won't hear me, so I sneak up behind her and whisper.

"Tell me what you need, Song Flower."

She whirls around to face me, a vision like always in the silver abaya that graces her frame.

Psalm

My wits are at their end when I hear a soft voice behind me. Soul is standing there patiently. Everyone else melts away.

"I need all these bags dropped at these locations with each of these cleaning schedules. I also need to make sure all these tools are accounted for with the bags."

"Say less. Where do you want me to go?"

"My brother Jazz is over there with all the materials."

He immediately went over to my brother. Soul has no idea how much he has just taken off my plate. It only took him three minutes with Jazz to start getting everything loaded up.

"Novali, make sure the emails go out with all the locations for each family. Here, take my laptop."

Novali is off, and that also relaxes me.

"People, people, please return to your previously scheduled programs and look out for emails to be sent in the next hour. Thank you for all of your patience."

Slowly, the crowd begins to disperse, and the air returns to my lungs. This is manageable. This is doable. Mom had screwed me this morning. She came down the stairs like she did nothing wrong.

We were sitting at the table having breakfast. It was surprising Mom wasn't at the table in the first place.

"Psalm, what are you doing at the table? You have a lot to do today."

Chyna, Novali, and I shared a look.

"Last time I checked, there was nothing on my schedule today."

"You didn't get my text last night? I have to run for the day, so you'll be in charge of the Kuumba cleaning projects."

"What!"

"Yes, you should pay more attention to your phone. Now, here, you literally have two hours to get all the assignments out to the families. At the very least, I have it all listed in these documents."

"Dad, she can't do this to me."

"I'm sorry, princess. We have to run down to Sacramento for the day. We can't afford to miss this meeting."

My rage turned back to my mother. "This is irresponsible. You are going to single-handedly ruin Kuumba for everybody."

"Psalm, watch your mouth when you talk to me. This is a part of your job, anyway. It's our turn this year."

"You should have told me this when I got here."

"Watch. Your. Mouth," she repeated.

"That's enough. Yes, your mother should have given you more heads up, but we weren't expecting this meeting to pop up. All of your siblings are on deck to help, and I am sure you can call on your friends. Do this for me, Princess," my dad added.

"Fine."

He tried to pull me into a hug, but I backed away. They had really done it for me this time. The entire table started talking once they left.

"Guys, please give me a second to sort this out. Then I'll let you know how to help me."

Now, we almost drowned. Something about Soul's whisper brought me back to the present. *I have the training for this. We can do this. All we need to do is get everyone organized.* I went back to the truck to see the box of phones someone had forgotten.

"Shit!"

It would be nearly impossible to coordinate without them. Jazz and Soul had started dropping things off at our checkpoints, so I had no way around. Thankfully, I see a Nation cop car and wave them down.

"Psalm, is everything okay?"

"Yes, I just need to drop these phones off, and I have no ride. Do you have a second?"

"Anything in the spirit of Kuumba," he says with a smile.

With luck, we can catch up to one of the guys, and they can take me around to the rest of the stops. Jazz was lingering at the first stop.

"What are you doing? Novali sent the emails out already. We have to haul ass."

"I can't find the box of phones."

The cop tosses Jazz the heavy box.

"Come on, we can move faster together," I add as he speeds out of the location.

It's a race against time. Mom has risked the entire family's reputation with her stunt.

"Psalm, don't be too upset with her."

"If this fails, it's on Mom, and the family reputation will be ruined."

"It won't be. We are all working as hard as possible to pull this off."

By the time we reach the last stop, Soul is trying to talk to an irate family.

"We need follow-up instructions. Clean-up was supposed to start ten minutes ago."

"I'm sorry, Mr. Perkson. Here is your phone, and just give me ten minutes to ensure everyone is in place. We appreciate your grace."

He grumbles away, making Soul chuckle under his breath.

"I got all the materials for my family. Is there anything else you need before I leave?" he asks.

"Abandon your family and keep helping me?" I joke before walking off to put out another fire.

When I come back to him, he hangs up the phone.

"Done."

"Soul, it was a joke. My siblings can have it covered."

"You guys look stretched thin as it is. You need the help, honey."

I smack him in the arm, and he laughs.

"Thank you, really."

"Any time," he replies.

His gaze is saturated with nervousness.

"Were you offended by the abaya?"

"Yah, no, it's gorgeous, and you got the size right."

"I pay attention."

"Clearly,"

The sunlight illuminates his soft gaze, and I want to trace his full lips with my finger. I want to kiss him again. The memory of their softness is imprinted in my mind. Jazz jogs over to us.

"Everyone is ready to go."

"Uh... that's perfect. You'll man our section. Soul will patrol sections 3-5, keeping in contact with me. Everyone has been distributed the same way. Let's eat this."

Jazz gives Soul a curious look. Jazz being in Soul's presence put my attention on all the rules he could be breaking by helping me.

"My apologies, but who are you?"

"Psalm and I share the same friends. My father also sent me over to get our supplies, and I noticed she needed some help."

Jazz eyed him for a second, then relaxed on the surface. "Thank you. We appreciate it, brother."

They shake hands, and we are off. Jazz drops me at my car, and the phone doesn't stop ringing most of the time that we are on the road with extra bags, resolving conflicts, and dropping donations. It has only been a few hours, and it feels like a few days. When the phone rings for the umpteenth time, a loud sigh escapes my lips.

"Yes,"

"Check your pockets," Soul says.

Sure enough, there is a green juice in my pocket.

"Oat milk matcha latte. It always gives me an energy boost."

"When did you do this?"

"Earlier, it was supposed to be my snack for later, but you need it more than I do."

"Thank you."

The silence was loaded like he had something on his mind. Was he also thinking about our night on the beach? Or what it would mean if we said yes to each other?

"Soul?"

"I'm still here."

"Why?"

"It seems like you do a lot for all the people around you, and it goes unnoticed. Not with me, and If I can help it, you will never have to struggle alone."

Jazz is on the other line, and Soul hangs up when he hears the beep.

I'm not dense, but it seems like there is more than one meaning to Soul's words.

Did he seriously like me? His hesitation to say what was clearly in his eyes in the garden and on his lips in the sand, makes me worry about his intentions. I'm not his type, and that is made clear by the way he wears his hair and the piercing in his nose. I could never have the courage to pierce something so out there. I had to fight my mom for my double ear piercings on each side and don't get me started on the half-shaved head and partial locs. Soul is a rebel, and it is known that rebels don't make good husbands, but should that even matter? Shouldn't the only two things that matter be how he treats me and if he serves Yah?

After we first met, I paid more attention to the things people said about him, but none of those things reflect how he has treated me since the moment I fell into his lap. He has been nothing but the perfect gentleman, not to mention he is such a handsome man. Soul is tall, dark, and stylish. Then there is his breathtaking smile and the way his locs shift into his eyes when he laughs. His energy allows me to relax, and I feel supported.

Being a background character in my family had left me with a lot less appreciation than my other siblings, especially from my mother. The drive today is proof of that very thing. Being the family representative in charge of one-fifth of our three-country three-state ecosystem and some of its most important parts is a lot. We are on the cutting edge with our research, yet my mother complains about me not being present for things like I spent all of my time in Bali eating and surfing. All the fixing I do for my siblings when I am home and halfway across the world goes unrecognized. So, for Soul to see me so plainly and take up as many mantles as he can for me makes my heart melt. From our first meeting to his help today, he has shown me he cares deeply for me. I feel the same way for him. The feeling knocks into my heart like a rush of wind. He saw me smoking and swearing. He saw me pious and poised, but he still wants me. The only thing missing is him saying the words, but because of this situation with Joa, he isn't going to say them.

We wrap things up cleanly and get thank-you packages and dinners sent to all the families who participated. After being interviewed on the news about our multi-county cleanup, I go home exhausted but still ready to challenge my mother. No matter what my dad had to say to me, my mother still owed me an explanation for her behavior today. This feels personal.

She is sitting at the kitchen table, eating cornbread and milk. It's a tradition for her. Everyone had taken the night off after the clean-up fiasco, so it's just us.

"Are you going to tell me what happened today?"

"You did your mother a huge favor, and she appreciates it."

"Mom, don't do that right now. Today was really hard for me, and we narrowly avoided a stain on our reputation and a huge disaster on our hands."

"Don't talk to me about our reputation when I'm the one who has been maintaining it for your whole life."

"Stateside. I handle all of our international relations, and you know better than anyone how much that could have been impacted by today."

"This is the job you wanted, honey."

"Don't go there," I scoff.

"Let's. You could have let Jazz do this job, but it's your passion, right? So what, you had to handle some stateside business. It's your job."

She is making it hard for me to keep my cool.

"You're right. You know what else? I don't think I am ready for marriage to Joa."

Mom's empty glass clanks down on the table.

"This again? I have met all your demands. Joa is adorable and kind, and he lives in Bali. You can keep living there and fulfill your responsibilities."

"Maybe this isn't about responsibilty. Maybe this is about love." As soon as the vulnerability is out there, I regret it.

"Love?" Mom questions.

"I don't love Joa, Mom, and I don't know if I can, but there is someone that's in my heart."

"Soul Niwibwe?" she mocks.

"Don't say his name like that!"

"Is there any other way to say his name when he is flighty and irresponsible?"

"You don't know him."

"You don't! When you met him at that party, I did my research on him."

How did she know about that?

"He spends all his time doing art and having sex with pagan women in New York. He is a joke, and you *will not* be his latest punchline," she snaps before storming out of the room.

Damn it. Soul doesn't seem like that type. His whole bad boy image seems like a farce, and I am going to prove it for myself. On Jiacom his post says he is watching the drone show with his friends, so that is where I'm heading. I need to get the truth. I don't want to take Mom's word for it, but I don't want to be blinded by love.

Soul is sitting on a bench, watching the colors play out in the dark sky. I sit next to him, taking in the show for a little while.

"What are you doing here?" he quizzes.

"Since we met, there has been something between us. Something romantic. Something good."

It almost set me in a panic to say the words.

"But there are some things I've been hearing about you. Like your penchant for pagan women. Is it true?"

He stared into his water bottle for so long that I was going to get up and leave.

"Yes, it's true, but I don't want you to know me for that."

"So was all of this so you could..."

"Of course not! Psalm, I would never disrespect you that way. I would never..."

"Then why didn't you tell me?"

"I want to be good for you. That's not who I want to be."

"How is that not who you are? That's who you were before your plane landed in LA."

"I have been figuring out who I am and have made some bad choices along the way, but that doesn't change how I feel for you."

"How do you feel for me? You haven't even said the words. Say them, and I'll forgive everything. We can move on from this if you say the words."

He didn't say anything else, and I can't take sitting here, and he never says them, so I went home.

This doesn't make my feelings for Soul go away. Mom's words don't wash away who he has been to me, but his not being honest made me question his character. I don't know if it should. Soul didn't owe me a word about his personal life, nor did I, but when he looked into my eyes on Nia night, it felt like I had betrayed him by being with Joa. The kiss we shared afterward made me feel like there is hope for us.

This is all so new to me. My life has never been complicated in this way. Joa should be enough. He is perfectly acceptable, and that had been good enough before, so why isn't it now?

When my eyes open in the morning, tears slide out of them. It's the last day of Kwanzaa. Imani. A day of worship. The most traditional day of Kwanzaa. Later tonight, we would dress in white and go down to the holy St. Victoria's church. The shaman would deliver a powerful sermon praising our dedication and love for the people. We celebrate the blessings of Yah and the blessing who we are to each other and our community. We celebrate love in all of its forms. There isn't much love in my bubble right now. I had never felt so alone.

A soft knock on the door made me tuck myself deeper into the sheets, hoping they would go away.

"I know you're awake," Novali calls.

I ignore her. She should go away anyway. In the last few days, we have not seen eye to eye about my marriage journey, and without us being on the same page, I feel even more alone.

"Psalm, get out of bed and talk to me."

"Go away, Novali."

"You are being immature about this."

"I get to be imperfect from time to time."

"That's not what this is about," she exclaims.

"Why are you still here?" I cruelly reply.

"Don't be a bitch with me because you're mad at Mom."

"Well, you're doing her bidding, so I'm considering y'all the same person."

"I just want you to be okay."

I sit up, tossing the sheets to the side and glaring at her.

"You have a funny fucking way of showing it."

"Is this about Soul?" she snaps.

All the strength drains from my voice as I realize.

"You told her."

Novali looks so guilty that she can't stand still for a second.

"Can you go? I have a day to get ready for."

Novali leaves defeated, and she leaves behind her guilt, but it is hard for me to be sympathetic to her. All Novali had to do was keep my secrets. It's not like Soul and I were making out in the streets. This is the first time I felt true love on my own. It is Novali's job to guide me through these exciting moments, yet she left me to figure things out by myself. Mom doesn't care about my feelings. She doesn't care about love. All she cares about is money and connections. She shoved my vulnerability back down my throat and basically told me to shut up about it.

No one is going to listen to me, but me, and that hurt to my core. The women in my life have abandoned me for whatever reason they see fit.

Mom came up the stairs as stiff as ever.

"Joa is here. You guys are going to have breakfast in the garden, go to the museum downtown, and have lunch."

"Whatever you say," I answer.

We go for a soft pink abaya today. The cream head wrap compliments it well, and I take my time getting dressed. Joa looks very handsome, sitting at the table in the garden and drinking his tea. There is a delicacy in his movement. He isn't in a rush. He is patient. Maybe I need some patience. With Joa,

Mom would never bother me again. I can just live my life. There is happiness to be found with a kind and patient man.

"Beauty is her name," he breathes, causing me to blush.

"Are you alright today?"

"Of course, we haven't done anything yet." I chuckle.

"I know. You just don't seem as vibrant as usual. I am wondering what the reason for that could be."

"It's been a long week. I can't wait to get back to Bali."

"I know what you mean. There is something about the water out there."

"Yeah, you catch the best waves."

He looks surprised. "You surf."

"Yes," I bashfully answer.

We spend the morning talking, and it's better than being at the breakfast table. Chyna has been staying with Abraham's family since her fight with Novali, and I can't blame her. It's easier than dealing with the real reason they are at odds. We promised each other the holidays would be easy, but they rarely were. Joa is a perfect distraction, and it is nearly disrespectful to label him as such. He is so much more than that. Joa has good jokes and interesting stories about his year in Antarctica or on the seas chasing the waves. He has an adventurous spirit, and we would never be bored together.

Still... he isn't Soul. Every time Joa laughs, I think about Soul's humor. Or what he would have said in response. He has saturated this process for me, and with his character in question, it should be easy to cast him off. I had been too rough on him, and he should know that, but Joa and I are going to be together all day. A part of me doesn't mind that. His company is nice to have. He is an anchor or a lighthouse, someone who you know will hold you down or guide you home. It's displayed clearly in his personality. It is in the way he holds his teacup and walks beside me. He is always the gentleman and patient with me. It's calming after the morning I had.

After the museum, we sit at a cafe enjoying baklava and coffee. The sun is shining. Brightly illuminating the red strands in his locs.

"Could you do this every morning with me, Psalm?" he quizzes.

Sit in this grace with him? Yes. It would be easy to be with Joa. It would be the most riskless path I could take, but for some reason, that made me panic. Would these normal days be enough?

"Of course, it would be easy to wake up next to you."

"I know you're concerned by the speed of this match, but they made a good choice for us. We can be happy together, and there is no rush. We can be engaged for as long as you want. No one is in charge of this relationship but you and me."

My fingers find his, and we share a glance in the direction of our chaperone. Yes, we can do whatever we want, and I don't have to make things difficult for us. Soul would be a difficult path for me to take, and I don't even know if he would be worth it in the first place. He still has not defined his true feelings for me. As much as I want to be with him, I need to know that he will do what it takes to be with me. I don't have the luxury of parents who will let me figure things out with him in New York. I have more risk than he does.

Dad always told me about our choices. They can make or break our lives. Mom has taught us to trust her because a mother knows best, and right now, it feels like my mother's choice could break my life. Joa and I don't feel like love. It feels safe. It feels normal. With Soul, I feel alive. Like I am on top of the world, but with Joa, I feel like I could be okay. Doesn't he deserve someone who wants to be more than just okay with him? Doesn't he deserve a shot at true love? And if I say I'm a good person, wouldn't it be on me to make that final choice for us?

Joa kisses my hand, and something turns in my heart. There is a possibility this could be love, but would I be willing to wait for that possibility?

Eight

Soul

OF COURSE, Psalm left me with my foot in my mouth. I don't want her to see me as someone dirty. The choices I made would make it inevitable. Men and women are expected to wait for marriage to have sex, and I have done the exact opposite of that. My body was for rebellion for a time. Sleeping with a pagan woman was a way to take my life back, and in the process, I had given up my reputation. I didn't think that would matter much, anyway. The look in Psalms' eyes told me it did. My actions seemed without consequence for so long. Now, it's all coming back to bite me. As soon as I gave her that abaya, my feelings were declared. I should have told her to truth. Psalm deserved to know what man she was falling for.

Psalm makes me want to be a better man. She makes me want to put my wild ways behind me and be someone worth loving. If she didn't know who I was, then we had a chance to be something fresh. As much as I try to lie, Isra has me pegged. I want Psalm more than anything in the world. She makes me feel worthy and free. Psalm wants me to put my feelings into words, but that makes it all real. I didn't know if I was ready for that but I do now. She would be worth leaving everything in New York behind. I have to align myself with that, and now, more than ever, it's important for me to become the person I am meant to be. My conviction may be too late. If my feelings and intentions aren't concrete, Psalm would move on with her life. As laid back as she is, Psalm is also very serious, she would not sacrifice her life for nothing. I am sure tonight would be the night they would make it official, and a few months from now, Psalm would have her engagement party to seal the deal. There would be no going back after that, and I am sure to spend the rest of my life wishing I had made my move.

The last night of Kwanzaa really happens at night. We usually do nothing during the day. Well, you do nothing if you are single. Potential matches spend the entire day together. Plenty of couples make their debut during the last night of Kwanzaa. The king and queen debuted during the Imani day of Kwanzaa as well, so tonight is the night, if there ever is one.

"Soul, come with me to pick up our tunics for the night," Dad says.

"Sure."

I toss on anything and follow him out the door. I keep my eyes off the windows. The last thing I want to see is Psalm having brunch with Joa. As hard as it is for me to admit, they look good together. She looks happy when she is with him, and she for sure doesn't look like she is thinking about me.

"Dad, you said you knew you were ready for marriage the first time you met Mom."

"Sure did."

"I'm ready."

His head whips in my direction at my admission.

"Do you know what you're saying?"

"Yes, she makes me want to be a better me for myself, but for her too."

"That is what love is supposed to inspire you to do. Who is she? Your Mom would want to get this off the ground right away."

We laugh.

"She's um...um... Psalm Rose."

He goes silent then, and that scares me.

"Son, I believe it's too late for her."

"Dad—"

"She's already found a match. Your mother and hers have an understanding. She isn't going to want to go against it."

"This is about her son being happy. Mom would do anything to make me happy."

"Not this. There are some things at work that you don't understand."

"Enlighten me."

"The Rose family isn't looking for love. Or to gain family through love matches. It's a different game for them than it is for us. Psalm's mother takes their marriages very seriously. You're a free spirit. You won't fit in there."

"I'm not looking to fit in. I am looking to love Pslam."

"Those things may be closer than you think," he responds.

All this time, they were pressuring me to get married, and now that I am ready, there's this pushback. I can't win for losing around here.

"Just tell me what I need to be, Dad, and I'll be that."

"Unfortunately, there is nothing more you can be."

"If it's not her, I won't ever get married. I won't ever come back to LA."

"Don't be childish in your thinking, Soul. Let logic be logic and emotion be emotion. This is not the place for you to be stubborn."

"It's my life. Shouldn't I get to be stubborn with it?"

"Not in this case."

"Your growth should be for you, not for Psalm."

"Can't it be both?"

"Not when you are making declarations like that."

"I don't want to hear any more of this," I grunt, getting out of the truck and slamming the door.

Dad can pick up the tunics alone, and I head in the direction of the house. Things aren't going to be easy, but anything is possible when you are in love. Dad is trying to sugarcoat things. There is more he isn't telling me. Mom will tell me.

By the time the house is in view, it's late afternoon. Mom is drinking tea in her office. Dad must have called her because she didn't look surprised to see me.

"So, you're ready to get married?"

"Yes, ma'am. I am."

"To someone you can't have. Are you trying to give me a heart attack?"

"No, I'm just trying to follow my heart."

"To a woman who is already spoken for."

"Not officially."

"Soul, what you are asking your father and me to do is bigger than you understand."

"Make me understand,"

She sighs. "The Rose family are not known for love marriages. They are known for strategic marriages. They make connections that benefit the family."

She pauses. "As close as we are, we have nothing she wants, but the Idrissi family does. Even if Psalm returns your affection, our empty hands plus your reputation would be a hard sell for the Rose family."

"So they marry their children off to the highest bidder. We aren't hurting for money. I can pay her bride price myself."

"It's not about the money. Mrs. Rose knows we have plenty of it. We just don't have anything that she wants. They choose marriages the children are comfortable with and that can raise their status."

Mom is trying to be gentle with me, but the gloves have come off. Psalm is out of my reach.

"So, I'm just supposed to let her go? I love her."

"Are you sure this is love, son?"

"Of course. I have never felt like this about anybody before. I'll take over the business. I'll move back to LA. Whatever it takes to be here for her."

"Let's think about this for a second. Step outside of your heart for a moment. Even if we could arrange something with the family, how would that even work? Psalm lives in a compound deep in the forest of Indonesia. Sometimes, there isn't even Wi-Fi out there. How do you think you would fare?"

"I—"

"Do you honestly think you'd survive in that forest? What

about Psalm? Do you think she would leave the comfort of that forest for New York or even come back to LA?"

"In Yah we trust, and through him, anything is possible. Ma, if I don't try, then I'll spend my entire life wishing it was her."

"Soul, you should take Psalm as your wake-up call. She opened your eyes to a life you thought you would never be able to live. What you should be looking at is a woman you can have."

"There is no woman if it isn't Psalm."

"Soul..." She sits back in her chair in exasperation.

"Ma, please, there has to be something you can do."

"Even my miracles are limited. You should go eat, sketch, and have a drink. Tonight is the last night of Kwanzaa, and in three days, you'll be back to your normal life. You won't even remember her next month."

Food is the last thing on my mind right now. No one had faith in me or Psalm because to assume she is forgettable is laughable. She is one of a kind, and no one will ever replace her. It wouldn't be fair what the next woman would have to live up to. It wouldn't be a life I would want for myself.

Tree is waiting for me when I get back to my room, which could be good or bad.

"What are you doing here? Shouldn't you be taking family pictures?"

"You know my wife made us take those pictures this morning. There is time to waste, so I wanted to check up on my boy."

"I'm fine."

"Come on, Soul, what's going on?"

"I want Psalm. My mom and dad know. I asked them to put a bid in for her marriage, and they refused."

"The Rose family isn't easy to get into. They are very strict on marriages."

"What have you heard?"

"It was rumored the oldest daughter, Novali, didn't want to get married until the mom made some arrangements. She was married within the year. Now, they have unlimited access to the farms in Paris, and it's paying off."

"Psalm doesn't want that."

"I hear she is getting engaged tonight, and people have seen her out with Joa all day. It's happening."

My pride keeps the tears at bay. We deserve each other. Could she be herself with Joa? Could she thrive with him?

"What am I supposed to do?"

"You have two options. One, you can let her go. Realize that there is a woman out there for you and that you can be home and be you. Or, you can admit your feelings to Psalm, and together, you can force your families to bend to your will. Her mother is not going to force her into marriage, and if Pslam pushes enough, the two of you can be together."

I am silent as I absorb his words.

"What if she doesn't feel the same way?" Tree quizzes.

"Then Psalm can go and be happy with Joa. She will never hear from me again. I won't fight with my dad anymore. I'll move back to LA and take over for him."

"Just make sure that this is about you and her, not just her."

I spend the rest of the day in my head. In the end, she deserves to know what her options are. My mom thinks I can't take it in Bali or that Psalm can't make it in New York, but mom is underestimating our love and will to make our lives together joyous. No matter what, I would be whatever Psalm needs me to be to be happy. There is one more opinion I need before I make my final decision.

Isra was in her room with the whole family. It is almost time to get ready, and being late isn't an option. She's wrangling my niece when I walk in. My niece screams in excitement, and Isra puts her hands on her hips.

"Can I have a minute with Isra?"

"Of course. Let's find your grandfather." Her husband says to his daughter.

They reluctantly leave the room, and Isra is nervous.

"You were right. I'm scared that all of this will end in disaster. My heart will be broken, and so will hers. I'm willing to risk it just for the chance to love her. Please, what can I do?"

"There may not be a rabbit I can pull out my hat this time. Her mother is running a tight ship. Unless you can convince her that Psalm's happiness is more important than making money, you don't have much of a chance, brother."

If Isra is saying that, then there is truly nothing I can do. Psalm is lost to me forever.

"At the very least, you know you are a man worth marrying and a person worth knowing. Don't lose what you found, even if you lose her."

That isn't enough for me because there is no marriage without Psalm. Isra was my last hope. If she doesn't have a way out then there truly is none, so I leave it alone and go to get dressed. This was supposed to be an uneventful trip home. Next year would have been my last year in New York. My dad and I would start putting things into place to put me in charge. This was supposed to be my last year home before things got serious, but it had gotten serious now.

The snow-white velvet tunic compliments my umber skin and white velvet pants. White diamonds decorate my septum piercing, watch, and earring. For the first time, looking good doesn't make me feel good. My emotions are out of control in a way unfamiliar to me. It makes me feel unruly and uncomfortable. By the time we are taking pictures before heading out, my hands are shaking. Dad looks over at me worryingly, another first.

We don't know what will happen when we make it to the church, but something is going to happen. Hopefully, it's something good. The entire church is lit up from every window. The light spilling through makes us all look like angels returning to heaven. There is a mingling session before the service where everyone gets to talk. Most people make their grand entrance during this time. I take a sip from my flask. I can't make it through this event dry.

If tonight is the night Joa would propose, Psalm and I will have to talk before then. That will be almost impossible, but she needs to know. If there is even the slightest chance she can return the feelings I have for her, we should explore it. This isn't the time of our parents. We don't have to court who they want us to court or marry who they want us to marry. My family is lucky. My parents got the chance to fall in love, but it doesn't always happen that way. Psalm's parents were arranged, but that time is over now. Psalm has the right to know that I am a choice for her.

My friends rallied around me. They don't have to say anything. Them being by my side is enough. Even with their support, I wasn't ready for their grand entrance. Psalm is a vision in her white silk abayas. She looks like an angel with each layer of draped fabric from her head to her feet. No one looks better than she does. Joa compliments her well, and they look like they belong together. I don't know if she looks the same way as me. She's holding onto his arm, and he is smiling at her. Diana rubs my back as they approach the shaman. He's not frowning at them touching, showing he approves of the union. The deal is basically sealed. All hope is lost, and once they walk into that cathedral together and sit next to one another there will be nothing she can do. Breaking her engagement and getting engaged to me would be scandalous. It could affect her job and potentially her life.

Typically, the mingling period lasts an hour, so the clock is ticking. Not only is Joa keeping her company, but Psalm's mother is watching her the entire time, not to mention her sister.

"Soul, do you want our help?" Xaevi asks.

"Yes, " I admit.

"Good, we have a plan," Diana says.

Soon, they find a way to distract everyone, and Psalm goes out to the church gardens alone. I slowly make my exit behind her.

"You look beautiful tonight, Song Flower," I compliment.

"You look as handsome as always," she replies, biting her lip.

"I should have been honest with you about the mistakes I made. You have changed me. Nothing about that life appeals to me anymore. I am in love with you, Psalm, and I want us to be together. I love you. I'm sorry it took me so long to say it."

"How can I trust you won't lie to me again? How can I trust this is how you feel?"

"You have my word on the grave of my ancestors. From now on, I'll be honest with you, and our love will be the most important thing for me."

The distance between us closes.

"I love you too, Soul, and I want you more than anything," she squeaks out. Psalm laces her fingers in mine. "You are creative, handsome, intelligent, and gentle. You see me."

Her soft cheek feels like clouds on my fingertips. Her lips aren't too far away. The thought of repeating our moonlight kiss is tempting.

"Psalm, just say the word, and we can make this happen."

Her face goes devastatingly sad, and she takes a step back.

"Soul, my mom will never let us be together."

"If you want me, then it won't matter what your mother says. I'm no slouch. Whatever you need, I will give it to you, and our families will love each other in time. It won't be easy, but nothing worth fighting for is."

The vertical gold line on her lips parts as she takes a step forward. Her light touch traces my bottom lip.

"I've never fought my mother for anything before," she whispers.

"Every day, I'll make sure I am worth the fight."

We are approaching dangerous territory. These touches are forbidden. There is not a husband and wife who would do this in public.

"If you like Joa and me, then think about it. If you think I'm not the best choice for you, then that's okay. I love you enough to want the best for you, even if it's not me."

My urges got the best of me, and I kiss her lips gently careful not to smudge the paint and go back to the party before we can be spotted. She loves me, too. We are in love with each other, but something is holding her back. Whether it's her standing up to her mother or the feelings she may have for Joa, whatever she wants, I will give it to her without a shadow of a doubt. I can't hide the smile on my face when I walk back in. My friends and siblings smile back at me. They know this smile means hope.

It's time for us to go into service. The entire cathedral is lit up in the colors of the Pan-African flag. Red and white roses decorate the pews and the pulpit. Strings of green silk dance and decorate the room. Psalm looks like a vision as she walks, but she doesn't walk in with her fiancé. She walks in with her sister. Joa doesn't show an ounce of confusion. He keeps his composure like always, but that is fine with me. He is the least of my concerns.

Mom pinches my hand to make me pay attention to the shaman.

He gives us a powerful sermon about prosperity, blessings, and the promised land. He preaches that we have done the work with Yah to create this growth for ourselves. This is the one night where no one is higher or lower than the other. Even the royal family sits in the front pew, eating up every word the shaman preaches. It's hard not to feel inspired by the convection of his words. We are more than worthy of Yah's love. We have done his bidding, and we continue to be examples of his forgiveness and love. Because of our combination of work and faith, we deserve the promise land we dwell in currently. Psalm's eyes never leave the pulpit, and she is one of the women who are invited up for additional prayer. It's like they can sense her dilemma. She is gracious and serious as they go through prayer together. I wonder if she is praying for me. Knowing Psalm, she is.

The sermon ends too soon, and we go to the royal hall for a closing Kwanzaa dinner. We then go to our homes and light the final candle in the kinara. We are invited based on our personal work with the royal family, so it's an honor. Many people don't get to meet the royal family directly.

When they walk the streets, they are always accompanied by the guards. Here, though, we are all the same person. Psalm and I are a ways away from each other at the dinner table. Of course, she is sitting next to Joa. He is very attentive and patient. It is like he thinks about every move he makes before he makes them. His calculating nature is interesting to me. The king interrupts us with a rousing speech and thanks us for all the work we do to make the Nation special, and we tuck into the decadent meal. I'm calm about the entire situation now. All my eggs are in Psalm's basket. If she truly is meant for me, then we will be.

Nine

Psalm

MOM HAD SENT HOME every spouse. It's the one night a year they return to their families. Of course, the children go with the women, and the immediate family lights the final candle on the kinara. It's a bittersweet moment for me. This holiday season will always hold a special place in my heart. This is the season I fell in love. So I will never regret this year. All of us go to get ready. Part of the reason this final moment is for the immediate family is the women are allowed to wear their hair uncovered. No one else can see our crowning glory.

My final outfit for the week is a sweeping lilac gown, complete with a cinched waist. My fingers expertly undo my two-strand twists, revealing gentle curls. A little moisturizing spritz completes the look. Chyna waltzes in while I'm doing my makeup.

"I never thought we would see the day you and Novali have beef."

"We don't have beef."

"You're not spending every second together, which is basically the same thing."

"We just haven't been seeing eye to eye. I... needed her, and she wasn't there for me."

"Both of you are flying home in two days, so you guys need to bury this."

Chyna advocating for Novali meant things must be bad.

"She needs to apologize."

"About Soul?"

"Mom knew nothing, and Novali told her everything. What happened to sister-to-sister confidentiality?"

"Let's go ask her."

Chyna grabs me by my elbow, and we go to Novali's room. She is on the balcony with the boys. She takes them to their room and we sit in the sitting room together.

"Look, I shouldn't be the voice of reason here. You're going back to Paris soon, and you're going back to Bali. We need to dead the beef between us."

"I'm not trying to fight with Psalm," Novali stresses.

"It's kind of hard to believe that when you told Mom my business."

"You don't understand how fragile your image is. If one person thinks something is going on with Soul, it would ruin you. I went to Mom because she can help."

"Psalm, can you understand that?" Chyna questions.

"Yes, and no. Novali, we should have had a conversation before you went to Mom. That's my whole point. When our parents are gone, we will be all we have. You have always toed the line, and I respected that, but this time you disrespected me."

"I'm sorry, but does it even matter now? You and Joa are going to get married."

"We don't know that for sure," Chyna interjects.

"I do. Mom told me he was supposed to propose at the church. We don't know why he didn't."

I know.

"Psalm, will you say yes?" Chyna asks.

"I'm not sure. Joa is a great man, Chyna. Mom did a good job picking him, but this is a huge decision, one that could affect the rest of my life. I don't know what I'm going to do."

I want to tell them about Soul's admission, and about all the ways he shown love to me. Novali has proven she can't be trusted, and pulling Chyna aside would raise Novali's suspicions. Music coming from down the stairs reminds me that it is time. The lights are dim. Candles guide us to the living room. For Kwanzaa, all the couches were gone and replaced with floor seating and towering displays, none more decadent than the ceremonial table. Each of the candles brightly illuminates the peaceful scene. Mom and Dad are already seated. They are holding hands. I take a deep breath.

The only thing on my mind is finishing out this sacred time. We sit in silence as each member of the family sits in order of their birth. Only Hebrew will be spoken from this moment on. Dad reads the holy scriptures for each day. His voice rose, reverberating off the high ceilings. When he got to the scripture for today, he made sure to make eye contact with each one of us. Finally, Jazz smashes two pomegranates, and we share the seeds, praying for one another. I light the last candle in the kinara, and we bow our heads in quiet prayer.

Tears come to my eyes during the prayer hour. There has to be a sign or something from Yah on which path I should take. It's hard not to panic at this moment. There aren't many choices that render me useless. It feels like I will lose no matter the choice.

Mom closes us in group prayer, and we pass around the last presents of the week. Dad goes to make each of our plates. Chyna hands me two boxes. One is small and blue. The first box is something she would give me, but the second box doesn't look like anything they would buy.

"Someone asked me to give this to you a few days ago."

Her eyes told me who that someone was.

"I was waiting for a reason to. Novali isn't the only one who wants to protect you," she whispers. Chyna touches my hand and goes to give Jazz her gift.

The box is made of velvet and decorated with embroidered flowers. Inside, the decorations continue, and nestled into the cloud fabric is a little guitar. It's made of blue wood and has one pink flower carved into the back. Each string is made of blue silk and fastened with gold clips.

The note in the box says: *For Little Psalm.*

I wiped away my tears quickly before Mom could see them. Soul is serious. It's a guitar for my inner child doll to play. I realize how close I let him get to me. This consideration is worth fighting for, and if I married Joa and tried to forget Soul, I would spend the rest of my life pining after him.

Novali comes to look over my shoulder. "It's beautiful," she whispers.

"It really is," Chyna whispers to the left of me. Both of them take my hand and silently lend me their love and their blessing.

Mom isn't going to budge, so I have to make a stand for myself. I have to do something she can't ignore.

We wrap up the meal together, then go our separate ways. Novali won't be here long, and Chyna will be back at Abraham's permanently. These last few days are sacred for us, but sometimes, you have to make sacrifices to get what you want. My fingers find Soul's Jiacom, and I type him a quick message. Hopefully, he will agree with me.

No one comes to this park anymore. It's on the fringes of our community. People see it as unsafe. Despite all the work we do for others, small prejudices still exist against them. They don't serve Yah. They don't adhere to the old laws, so we must keep ourselves separate from them. We are using that prejudice to our advantage tonight.

As he walks through the gates, the blue lights bathe him in its cool glow.

"Psalm, what are we doing he—"

My lips envelop Soul's, and he hesitates for a moment before leaning into the kiss. It is just as magical as our first kiss.

"I want this with you more than I want anything else. Whatever it takes."

Soul leans forward like he wants to kiss me again, then looks around.

"I'll never get tired of kissing you, but you know we have to be careful. You have been promised to another man, and the last thing I want is for you to get hurt," he reasons.

"Damn that promise. We can go. We can be alone until our

families realize we're serious. We can force them to let us live in love," I counter.

Soul looks torn. "Psalm, I can't take you away from your family and all the things you love. My feelings for you are more than romantic. I care about you so deeply that your happiness is my first concern."

"Soul, don't stop hearing me now. Without you, I won't ever know happiness. My mother gave me away when she didn't listen to me. Let's be together."

He pulls me into a sizzling kiss that makes my knees weak. It is the first kiss that makes me feel like flying.

"I know where we can go. Pack your things and meet me here in two hours."

Soul scribbles down an address, and we go our separate ways. My heart is in my throat. My head is dizzy with freedom, with possibilities. For so long, my mom has controlled everything I do. She is like the bank to my river, dictating the places I could ebb and flow. This feels like taking my life back. This feels like being the best of Psalm *for* Psalm. My only regret would be wasting the little time I have with my sisters. My plan is we will be away long enough for Mom to see I won't back down. Soul and I are risking more than our relationship. We could be risking our lives. An unmarried Nation woman running away with a man is blasphemous and goes against everything Yah stands for, yet I believe in my heart that Yah wants my happiness more than anything in the world.

COFFEE JONES

I stay in my room for a moment when I arrive home, hoping everything will work out and I will be getting ready for my wedding here one day. Mom comes into the room while I'm packing. A soaring couch cushion saves me from her seeing the half-packed bags.

"Psalm, is everything okay?"

"Of course. Why wouldn't it be?"

"Joa told us he was going to propose to you tonight, and he didn't."

"Hopefully, he comes around soon. If not, we laid a great foundation, so it'll happen eventually," I offer.

"So, this Soul business is over with, and you are ready to marry Joa?"

"Yes, you are right about Soul. It is never going to work."

She looks relieved.

"For what it's worth. If he would have had his head on his shoulders, I would have considered it."

I pull my mom into a hug, and she kisses my forehead and cheeks. No matter what, we still love each other, and that will never change, at least not for me.

She leaves my room and then claps off the hallway lights as she goes. Unfortunately for her, this Soul business will never be over.

Once I'm sure the house is quiet, I go out to the balcony. Right next to it is an easily climbable tree. It doesn't take long for me to gracefully land on my feet and start my walk over to the meetup spot. Soul is waiting when I approach. We silently walk around the corner, slipping out of the community limits. A car is waiting, and Soul talks to the man as he climbs out, then throws my bags in the backseat.

"Let's go," he calls, opening the passenger side door.

The man waves as we drive away. Soul put his hand in mine, and I get my sign. There is no anxiety, no worry, just pure peace. No matter what, this is going to work out. We are going to be okay.

"What's the destination?" I ask.

"Punta Mita. There are some nice beaches down there, and it's far away enough that they won't come looking for us, but it's a long drive," Soul answers, smiling.

"More time for us to spend together." I smile back.

Soul's scent fills the car and makes me feel warm and fuzzy. When my head rests on his shoulder, he kisses my brow.

"Do you think this is going to work?"

"I don't know, but if it doesn't work, we didn't give up on each other. That would have been my one regret, wondering if we could have made it happen and if you're happier without me."

"Well, we won't have to wonder now," I add.

Before long, my eyelids get heavy, and I curl up into a ball and then drift to sleep.

The soft sunlight in my eyes wakes me. Based on the trees and flowers rolling by, we have to be halfway to Mexico by now.

"Soul, did you sleep?" I question.

He looks weary.

"Not yet. We should get further away first."

"Pull over, let me drive."

"You know how to drive?"

"My grandma taught me. Don't tell my mother." I chuckle.

"I can make it for a few more hours."

"Please, you can barely keep your eyes open. Pull over."

Without another word, he pulls over, and we quickly switch sides. It is jarring driving on the right side of the road, but it isn't too bad. Soul gets comfortable in the passenger seat and almost immediately falls asleep. He looks... at ease as if he had a wall up the entire time, and the only place he can let his walls down is in his sleep. I have to remind myself to keep my eyes on the road. He is a work of art.

I wish I hadn't left my phone behind. I want Novali to know about my first real kiss, and every kiss after. I want her to know that they were with a man who loves me. We had left almost six hours ago. Dad has been up for hours at this point, and he has already discovered me missing. It is the first morning after Kwanzaa, and he always brings me peppermint tea. We'd talk about the future, my visits home, and his visits to me and grandma. He will be so scared and worried, but I am only doing what he taught me. We do everything asked of us. I keep chaste. My abayas are always traditional, my Hebrew sharp, and my accolades plentiful. My parents and community never have to worry about me embarrassing them. I am always the perfect daughter, and Mom never sees me unless I step out of that role. She loves us, but we are still pawns to her. Not one of us has told her no, and before Soul, I would've done whatever she asked.

I give my life to Yah. I submit to his will, the will of my parents and my king. When would my will matter? When do I get a say? Marriages last a very long time in the Nation. We hardly see divorces. My parents have been married for twenty-eights years at this point. So, being married is a big choice, and it should be left to me. The value of someone's offer shouldn't matter, if it doesn't align with me. I have the final say. I thought I was choosing Soul when we ran away, but I am really choosing Psalm. A huge grin spreads across my face. It feels sinful to put my choice above Yah's, but it also feels liberating. I don't know which feeling matters more.

Soul

This has to be a dream. No woman can be this perfect. No, she is beyond perfection. Psalm is... holy. We had driven for nearly a day, which felt like a few hours. From guilt-sharing fast food to taking turns driving, we had an experience together. We should be feeling the effects of our decision. We should be panicking. However, the more time we spend together, the more this feels right. Psalm shakes my shoulder as the ocean comes into view.

"We made it," she sings.

Psalm's joy is infectious, and we dance together as we pull into the villa. Just in case, I keep a couple of off-the-record favors. I have a very high-profile place in the Nation, and things happen. I've heard whispers about what our legacy is truly built on, so I have to make sure as a man my shit is secure. The villa sits on the ocean miles of sandy beaches not too far from where we will be.

Psalm is hoping this will wake her mother up to her desires, but I am more realistic than that. Our families can see this as the ultimate form of disrespect and disown us. We can also be dismissed by the royal family. If Psalm is found not to be innocent, she could even lose her life. None of this is lost on her, but she chooses to be optimistic, and I will not take that away from her.

"Soul, this place is beautiful."

"It's not the only thing."

Her gaze locks on mine, and suddenly, her innocence is the only thing on my mind.

"How about we check out the ocean?"

She quietly nods, walking in the direction of the bathroom and then taking off toward the ocean.

"I bet I'll make it first!" she yells as she runs.

"Cheater!" I call, following her into the cold water.

"Ahh!" she laughingly screams.

The water shocks me awake. My arms wrap around her waist. Her lips are soft and wet as we kiss.

The wind whips the water around us. Psalm's skin glistens in the bright light. A lap of the wave takes her head wrap with it, and the wind pulls it out of its bun, causing her curls to tumble out. The sight freezes me in place. The light highlights each individual gold and brown curl. They tumble into the water, causing her to hold on to me tighter. She catches me staring.

"What?"

There are no words that can convey the awe I feel. "Let's get out of the cold, baby."

I kiss her nose, and we walk up the beach together, laughing about the sand sticking to our toes.

"Wait a second," Psalm says. She comes back to the beach with my camera and a vial. "We should save the sand. It's our souvenir," she mumbles, scooping the sand.

Once she is done, she strikes a pose.

"Come on, artist man. Get my good side."

"All your sides are good," I comment.

She drops her pose, and I get the candid shot.

Music drifts from the main areas of the resort, and Psalm pulls me into her arms.

"Dance with me, handsome."

My hate for wet clothes doesn't matter. The rumbling in my stomach doesn't matter. Psalm's smile matters more than anything. Watching her wet curls twirl in the waning sun matters. Once the music fades, I tug her inside.

"Get comfortable. I'll take care of the food."

Moments later, the shower starts, and I release a breath.

One step at a time, Soul.

That first step is dinner. It feels like a night for easy things. Guac and chips, some tacos. I even order us some margaritas. We will need them. The villa only has one bed. Thankfully, there are some couches in the living room. I don't trust myself in the same bed with her. That look in her eye isn't helping, either.

I take my shower in the second bathroom. The steam and distance give me a chance to think clearly. My art is definitely on hold at this point, as well. I chuckle at the thought of my manager blowing my phone up, trying to reach me. I know my mom is freaking out. Isra is pissed, Tade is amused, and my dad, well, he would be disappointed when he discovers Psalm missing too, but they have forced our hands with this. Psalm and I are grown-ass adults. We can make our own choices, and nothing feels bad about this one.

When I finish my shower, Psalm is sitting on the bed. Her legs are crossed under her powder blue abaya. To my dismay, she has wrapped her hair again.

"These tacos are delicious," she moans, offering me a bite.

Psalm has this look as I take a bite of the taco. It's hard for me to look away. This is a side of her I haven't seen before, and it makes me aware of things I push to the back of my mind, like the way her abayas subtly outlined her curves, delicate pout, and sensual eyes. It could just be Mexico getting to me.

I lay my head on her lap, and we watched *The Fresh Prince of Bel-Air*. The heat is comforting. Everything is — the blankets, the warm lighting, the glow from the TV, and the soft material of her abaya against my cheek.

"Soul?"

"Yes."

"Are you sure we are going to be okay?"

"Without a doubt," I whisper back.

She kisses my locs, which makes me feel a little guilty because there is a high chance we won't be. Still, I can't think about that now. It would be criminal not to live in the moment. Soon, the night went on, and I slid out of the bed.

"Where are you going?"

"To sleep on the couch."

"There is plenty of room in the bed with me."

"I don't think that is a good idea."

"Why not?" she naively inquires.

The silence between us colors her cheeks with blush.

"Well, I'm well-behaved, and it...would be nice to... sleep next to you."

She hits me with puppy dog eyes, and I melt.

"Well, as long as you're behaving."

Psalm goes around turning off lights before we do our nighttime routine and slip into bed together. Sex is the last thing on my mind as she settles into my arms. A sigh escapes her lips as her head rests on my chest. Psalm feels safe with me. Safe enough to cuddle into my arms. That intimacy is worth more than pleasure from sex could ever be. I never want to let her go.

"I love you, Song Flower."

"I love you more," she whispers in Hebrew.

Ten

Psalm

SLEEP HASN'T TAKEN me like that in eons. Walking up in Soul's arms is like waking up on a cloud. Or after you've had four tequila shots and slept fully clothed. After you've run all day and night through the park, then have a good dinner. It's refreshing. I needed this space away from what being Psalm has become. I am trapped in my ambition and rebellion, but this feels like maturity, like a responsibility you look forward to. The waves in the distance call to me, and I remember the surfing station we passed on our way into the resort.

"You want breakfast?" he asks as I hop up.

"No, I want to catch some waves. They look good."

"At least eat an apple or something," Soul chastens.

"I'll eat when I get back," I reply before brushing my teeth.

My wet suit goes on easily, and soon, my board is cutting through the waves. A part of me is waiting for our first fight.

Everyone says if you can survive that, you can survive anything. Jazz would call me a cynic. I miss him so much. He's worried, but he won't let it show. He will be angry but will keep his composure. Dad has raised him to be our protector, the one who could step up and run the family if he left us, which includes controlling the emotional and mental health of the family. That's why Jazz is always my hero. He would want to be my hero now. That makes me tear up, mess up my balance, and fall off my board.

Perhaps we should have given more thought to this. Jazz's sadness would be in his posture, his worry in the arch of his brows. I should've told them something before I left, but he wouldn't have understood.

Soul comes to the edge of the water and watches me crash out in another wave. My mind isn't in it, so I float back to the beach and toss the board on the sand. As soon as Soul is close enough, I yank him into the water.

"For the love of Yah!" he shouts with a laugh.

Our lips find each other, and he doesn't stop kissing me for a while. This is addicting — the warmth of his skin, the lightness of his voice, the sun beaming down on us. We could stay here forever. We could roam the earth as nomads, hunting and gathering like our ancestors.

"This is what my heaven would be," I whisper.

"This is my promised land," he replies.

My heart nearly pounds out of my chest as the words leave Soul's mouth. It's a thrilling thought. No more head wraps, abayas, limitations on jobs, and driving. No more submission to my parents or being chastised because I want my own place. Still, I could never leave the Nation forever. That means leaving my dad, mom, and siblings, missing birthdays and funeral pyres. My nephews would grow up without me. I know Soul could never throw his family away either, but maybe we already have.

Surprisingly, he doesn't rush me out of the water. We hold each other occasionally, sharing a kiss.

"You want to try surfing?"

"Me! No, I have the balance of a newborn horse."

"It's not that hard," I say, rolling my eyes.

Eventually, Soul is convinced, and he proves his statement right. It takes forever just to get past the balancing part. I decide not to push or tease him too far.

Breakfast has passed when we walk up the beach. In the living room are all the pieces for a guitar. There are various colors for each piece. I notice them after my shower. Soul passes me a plate filled with fruits, raw veggies, and a few grilled oysters before sitting back on the floor.

His back muscles flex under the thin t-shirt he wears as he works with the raw wood. The thought of his gift flashed in my mind.

"I never got to thank you."

"For what?"

"My Nia gift. Little Psalm appreciates it more than you know."

"If you didn't choose me, I still wanted you to have something meaningful to remember me by," he whispers back, never stopping the motion of his hands.

"We would never forget you, anyway."

Soul keeps working, and I keep watching him. He knows

when to be gentle and when to be hard. He is patient as the process wanes on.

"How long does it normally take you to make one?"

"Three weeks, but it can be longer depending on the demand. I just started this one."

"Can I help?"

Soul pulls me into his lap off the arm of the couch and guides my hands with the whittling knife. It was different from doll making. The strokes are broader. There is a lot more patience in this process. Once he is preparing for a break, I straddle his lap. Watching him create causes a flash of desire in me, so when I kiss him, there is something involved. My body molds to his. We almost become one. Soul's manhood under his linen slacks greeted me, and another feeling rose in my belly.

"Psalm," he moans as I slip his tongue in my mouth.

Soul's hands grip my cheeks, and his kisses trail down my neck. He picks me up in one swoop, alternating between kissing my lips and my neck. Soul tosses me on the bed and walks away abruptly. The door to the beach closing gently behind him as he goes. I sit up, panting. Deep breathing helps put me at ease. He is right to hold back. Our feelings can't push us to make decisions that go against our beliefs.

I turn my attention to the plate and put on a random show. It's my fault. I pushed us both, but not wanting him on that level is hard. He makes every part of me sing. Soul's beauty isn't lost on me. He towers over me. Those deep brown eyes tell stories, and when he licks his lips, I melt. It dawns on me then. This is lust. This has never been an issue for me before, but it's so consuming. Once I sat in Soul's lap, I wanted him in the worst way. I wanted him to make a woman out of me. Laws be damned.

He quietly returns and pops a grape in his mouth.

"I'm sorry, but you were pushing me to my limits."

"Yeah, that was on me. Something came over me. That hasn't happened before."

He smirks. "I don't know if I should be scared or honored."

"Perhaps a little of both."

He quietly chuckles.

"I don't know how things are going to end, Psalm. I want to make sure that no one can question your virtue. That is the last thing you deserve."

"I understand, but just so you know, if anyone deserves my virtue, it's you."

"Stop talking like that," he groans, falling back on the bed with a pillow over his face.

"I'm sorry, but it's true, especially since we are getting married, anyway."

"You don't know what's going to happen."

I frown at him. "Are you saying you don't want to get married?"

"We have broken a lot of laws, and at the very least, I want to ensure we don't break the most important one. What I am saying is that you are too optimistic."

"One of us should be. I know all our realities, but there is no point in dwelling on them. I was well aware of the risk when I left my phone in the bush," I argue.

He won't look at me.

"Love matters more." I probe.

"So, you are okay with knowing you won't be able to do your job again. Your family has spent decades cultivating those biomes. You can just leave them," he argues back.

Something else is going on here. Soul isn't going to make this about me.

"Losing access to my ancestral work would be devastating, but this isn't about that. You don't feel like you're worth it, but you are. Don't put your insecurities on me."

"Insecurities? That's rich coming from you."

"What the fuck is that suppose to mean?"

"Your entire image is cultivated to keep people out. Is it because you think they won't like what they see? Is that because you don't live up to the Nation's standards?"

"This is not about me!" I shout.

"Why shouldn't it be?" he shouts back.

"Because I know what I want. I always do. The problem is you don't. You didn't have to do this with me, Soul. You could have said no."

I throw a pillow at the back of his head and storm out of the room.

I watch sand slide through my fingers while sitting on the beach. The moon mocks me with its brightness. My heart is in my ass, and embarrassment is on my mind. Mom was right. Soul isn't secure. He is scared, rightfully so. We have taken the biggest risk in the world, which isn't lost on me. I guess he thinks it is because I'm calm about it. My dad says panicking doesn't solve problems, especially the ones we create for ourselves. We asked for this when we got in the car and drove twenty hours to a beach. Soul asked for this when he kissed my hair in the ocean when he pulled me close as we slept.

Soul is not going to make me regret this or make me color

this moment gray. He can cry on his own about our sacrifices since it's clear he didn't think them through in the first damn place. As for my image, it has to be about keeping people out because when I make choices, I am sure about them. I stand on my morals with all ten toes. That's too much for people, so my image is deep enough to communicate my cause and nothing more. Somehow, Soul sees through all of that. He sees the real me and treasures her. That's how I know he is worth the wrath waiting for me at home. If he doesn't think he is good, none of this is worth it, and I am wasting my time. You can't love someone into loving themselves. You can't love someone into being confident in themselves. There has to be a flame for you to stoke.

A chill runs through me, and I shiver a little. A warm blanket covers my shoulders, and a perfectly wrapped joint and lighter hit my lap. Soul's retreating frame meets me when I turn around. *How can he not see what I see?* It hasn't dawned on me how long it has been since I smoked, but he knew. Soul is good. He is the person that will help you if have a flat tire. He's the stranger in line behind you who'll pay the difference for your groceries. Sometimes a person is too good to recognize it in themselves. The lit end of the joint illuminates the space around me. My stubbornness keeps me on the beach for a long time. It's childish, but I don't want him to win. Soon, my tired body makes its way to the couch, and sleep takes me.

In the morning, I roll over deeper into the covers and am surprised my body doesn't hit the floor. Soul is tucked in next to me, still sleeping. A vague memory of him carrying me to bed flashes through my mind. I tuck my body closer to him, stirring him awake.

"Good morning, Song Flower."

"Good morning, my love," I answer.

"I apologize for the things that came out of my mouth yesterday. I acted mostly on emotion when we ran away together. It wasn't wise not to think all of this through, but that doesn't mean I don't stand by my choice. The chance at love with you is better than no chance at all." Soul kisses me on the forehead and pulls me closer.

"That is important for me to hear. I was worried that you regretted me."

"Nothing will ever make me regret choosing you. Nothing." He tilts my lips to meet his. "By the way, of course, I want to marry you. I'd marry you today if you want."

We share more kisses before ordering breakfast, eating fresh melon bathed in sunlight.

It takes a lot of convincing to get Soul back on the board after breakfast, and he does a lot better than I thought he would.

"Let's go out," he suggests.

"Yeah, it's not like anyone knows us down here."

"Exactly."

He laughs, watching me run out of the water to get ready.

Soul looks so handsome in his white linen suit that we barely make it out the door. We ride ATVs and go horseback riding before strolling through the city hand in hand.

"So, do you truly think you can live at the compound with me?"

"It'll be a piece of cake."

"We don't eat meat out there, only have Wi-Fi twice a week, and spend most of our days outside."

He pauses before replying, making me giggle. "Well, it could be good for my art." Soul surprisingly wraps his arms around my waist. "Nothing matters as long as I'm with you."

He kisses me on the forehead, and we fill up on street food before going back to the villa.

"We should watch the sunset on the beach tonight," he suggests.

When we open the door, a man is standing in the living room.

Eleven

Soul

THERE IS no disappointment on his face. In fact, his expression is clear. That is scarier than anything. My arm keeps Psalm from running off.

"Dad."

"Soul," he responds.

The revelation makes Psalm relax a little, but we can both sense that she is still scared, so Dad smiles at her.

"Miss Rose, I'm going to take my son outside for a chat. Don't worry, he will be back."

Psalm has a death grip on my hand, and the look in her eye said she has no intention of letting it go.

"It's okay, honey. I'll be right back."

She reluctantly walks away from us, looking over her shoulder as she goes. Dad heads outside without another word, taking a seat in the chair on the patio. He won't even look at me.

"Soul, what have you done?"

"I made a choice for myself."

"And for me, your mother, Psalm, and her family, too. You made a choice for all of us."

"I didn't make Psalm come with me."

"No, but you drove her down here. You are the man in this relationship. That means you set the tone. You make the most important choices. If you told her to stay, she would've stayed."

"I didn't want her to. I want to be with her. You and Mom won't help me, and her parents won't help her. We chose for ourselves because these are our lives."

He chuckles sadly. "You want to be with her? That's your justification. Son, when you become a husband the most important thing is for you to do right by your wife."

"I am doing that."

"Are you? Let's see. You gifted Psalm an abaya, knowing how personal a gift that is. You spent unchaperoned time with her. You lured her away from her fiance. Took her, an unmarried Nation woman, to an entirely different country without marrying her, and that's just the tip of the iceberg. I would have even accepted a shotgun wedding. Can't you see? The moment she steps back into our streets, they will whisper behind her back. She will be lucky to get married now."

He is making valid points, but so am I.

"She won't have to worry about marriage because I intend to marry her."

"You think her family will accept you now? You took their unmarried daughter to an entirely new country against their will. If they thought you were a troublemaker before, they think you are the antichrist now."

"It doesn't matter what they think as long as Psalm wants me."

"It matters when they control all the things she holds dear. She can marry you, but I guarantee her mother will force her to step down. She'll lose her suite in their home and more than likely won't be allowed contact with her siblings. She will only have you. Is that the life you want for her?"

"I want her to have her own life. She should be able to choose whatever she wants."

"You're right. She should be able to, but unfortunately, these big choices aren't just up to her."

My head drops into my hands.

"Soul, I know you love her, but when you love someone, you must do what's right for them, even if that means leaving them."

"She'll never forgive me," I whisper.

"Some things are more important than forgiveness."

"Dad, I will come home. If you advocate for this marriage, I will give up art. I will run the family business. I will be the eldest son you have always wanted."

He surprises me by pulling me into a hug.

"Oh, Soul, you are already the eldest son I have always wanted. You are brave, smart, and kind. A father couldn't ask for more. I know you didn't make this choice out of maliciousness. You made it out of love. All I ask you to do is make another choice rooted in love *and* logic. Psalm's family and I have managed to keep this under wraps. People think she's on a last-minute wildfire project. Her potential fiancé will still marry her. We can all pretend like this never happened. When you go to sleep at night, you'll know you made the right choice as a man and as a man who loved a woman."

"*Loves*, that'll never go away," I counter.

"I wouldn't expect it to. I'll leave you guys to have a moment alone," he says, walking down the beach.

My feet can barely support me. The last thing I want to do is leave my baby. She has become everything to me, but Dad is right. I ruined any connection I could have made with her family by bringing her here. Psalm talks so passionately about her job. She thinks she can live without it, but she would miss it every day. Her research, the difference she is making. Her siblings mean more to her than anything else in the world, and she would miss them, too. All the things that made her Psalm would fade away from her. She would become a shell of the woman I love. That is the last thing she deserves.

"How did it go?" she asked, eating guava.

She is so beautiful it hurts.

"We have to go back."

"Your dad struck a deal?" she asks with excitement.

"No, you... have to go back to Joa."

Her face falls, and she jumps up from her seat.

"What are you talking about?"

"Your mom is right. I'm not good for you, Psalm. With me, you won't get the life you deserve, and it would be cruel of me to deny you that."

"Soul, please don't do this."

"I should've done this a long time ago. We never should've come here."

"What do I need to do... what?" she cries.

My thumb catches her tears.

"Baby, this is on me. There is nothing we can do."

"Is this about my family? Damn them! I don't want to leave you. Please," she begs.

"This is about no one but us. Joa is the best choice for you. I belong in New York, running away from my problems. You belong in Bali."

Psalm slaps me.

"You don't get to tell me where I belong! I get to choose! It's my life! I choose you!" she shouts through her tears.

I pull her into my arms, kissing her passionately. We melt into that kiss. She holds me so tight it makes me start crying.

"Please, please, please," she whispers in my ear.

"I'm sorry, baby, I love you. I love you. I'm doing this because I love you," I sob.

I could feel my dad's presence in the living room. Psalm resists me pulling out of her arms.

"You should pack," I whisper before turning around.

"I won't wait for you! If this is you self-sabotaging, then it'll be on you. I won't wait." Psalm insists.

I walk over to Pslam, sliding her wrap down enough for me to kiss the hair on her head.

"Don't."

She crumbles onto the bed, the quiet cries eroding my heart.

"I love you too," she declares.

"I love you more," I whisper under my breath.

My legs barely carry me out of the room.

"You did the right thing," my dad assures me as I pass him.

Nothing about leaving Psalm crying feels right. It is cruel to think so.

I thought they would wait until the morning to leave, but after a while, the sound of suitcase wheels on the wood grabbed my attention.

"We have a flight to catch back."

"Tonight?"

"Time is of the essence."

Psalm does everything she can to not look at me, but regret wouldn't eat me up. I am firm in my choice this time.

"Get home safe," I choke out.

Every other word feels like it would be too much. Psalm doesn't respond as Dad takes her bags.

"You should drive back. It'll give you time to think," he advises.

Dad isn't asking. This is going to be the start of a long list of punishments. It doesn't matter. She is worth anything I will endure. As soon as he leaves with Psalm, everything is cold. Finally, my body gives into sorrow. The tears come on their own. *I miss her.* It feels like someone has taken the wind from my lungs. I am almost in a state of panic. How long will her absence wound me like this, and will it ever feel like I did the right thing?

Psalm

Mr. Niwibwe is very kind and gentle with me. He doesn't talk to me on the drive to our flight, at the airport, or on the plane. There is nothing to say, anyway. They were so worried about what my family would think of him that we didn't stop to think about what his family would think of me. Soul is a troublemaker, yes, but outside of Nation borders. He doesn't cause the family problems, yet because of me, he has done just that. They could despise me as much as my mom despised him. It makes me chuckle to think of the mess we made for ourselves. My heart aches when I think of Soul's laughter or what he would have said.

Those days in Mexico feel like a distant dream. A beautiful, blissful dream of swell waves and wet kisses. *Oh, Soul, why did you have to leave me?*

"Miss Rose?" Soul's father prods while driving me home.

"Yes, sir?"

"I have not expressed my disappointment in you because I am sure you already know, but I will ask one thing of you. Forget my son. Soul is the gentle spirit you fell in love with. He's a bleeding heart. He will always love you, but I don't want that to derail the rest of his life. Get married, move on, and keep him as a memory," he advises.

Mr. Niwibwe parks in front of the door with no malice in his expression as I get out. Usually, my heart would be dripping in fear, but my love is lost to me, and the cause of it is inside. I am not a child anymore. It's time for me to truly stand up for myself. The living room is cold when I step into it. Everyone is waiting for me, but I am not in a greeting mood. Mom ran up to me for a hug, but I took a step back.

"This is all your fault," I snap.

"My fault? I'm not the one who ran away to Mexico with some hoodlum."

"Cut the high and mighty act! Soul isn't like that, and I figured that out for myself. He wanted to be with me, but of course, you twisted your precious *connections* to get what you wanted like you always do!" I shout.

"Psalm, don't be so selfish! Your choice had the potential to destroy this entire family!"

"Because of you! Because you wouldn't let us be together! I ran away because you left me no choice!"

"Everyone calm d—"

"Jazz, stay out of it," I hiss.

"Psalm, I am your mother. I know what's best for you. Soul is not what is best for you. The decades I have over you in age gave me a lot more time to figure it out what is."

My mind went dead calm.

"Since you have it all figured out, watch this."

I turn on my heels and head toward the stairs.

"Is that a threat, young lady?" Mom demands.

"No, it's a damn promise. I'll marry Joa, just like you want, and I'll stay in Bali just like I want. We will never see each other unless we have to. You'll have all the things you figured out."

"Psalm, that's too far," Novali adds.

"Oh, for the love of Yah, shut the fuck up, Novali!"

"Absolutely not!" Dad roars.

Damn it, I can't stop my tears.

No one follows me up the stairs. I go straight to packing. It's time for me to go home, anyway. My eyes land on Soul's abaya. I can't hold it in any longer. The sobs wracked my body, almost turning into wails. I shouldn't have said that to my sister. I should've fought for Soul. Everything is a mess. My heart is in pieces. Air catches in my lungs, the room starts spinning. How broken is too broken? Soul has taken all the warmth in the world away from me. There will be no grand love for me without him. It doesn't matter who my husband is if it isn't him. It doesn't matter where I am if he isn't with me. Soul sees something out of my view. He saw a life of me being miserable, so he let me go, believing he was saving me from that moment, but he pushed me into it.

I run out to the balcony and light a long-forgotten joint. I swing my feet over the edge, balancing on the thin railing. I thought Mom would put it all to the side for me. That she would trust my choice and encourage me to be happy, so it hurt me the most that she doesn't care about what I want. There are too many emotions swirling through my head. What did I have to do to get her to show me she loves me? She celebrates Jazz and praises Novali. She babies Chyna and coddles Chanson. I never complained about any of it, even the few times I did, she never heard me. Mom is always the most serious and the hardest with me. I could never figure out why.

The crisp night air ruffles my dress. It would be nice to join the night in flight, to disappear into the fabric of space and time for a little peace.

I will apologize to my sister. Novali doesn't deserve my wrath. As soon as I said it, guilt-wracked me. Novali was supposed to be in Paris days ago, but she waited for me. She was worried about me, and I had given her my anger.

"Psalm, get down from there!" Novali yells.

I turn in surprise and almost lose my balance, but she pulls me back onto the balcony.

"You came after me?"

"Of course, we've both said things, and honestly, none of us are squeaky clean in this conflict."

"I'm so sorry. You didn't deserve that."

"Thank you for the apology. I'll accept it after you make it up to me," she adds.

"Noted."

"How was Mexico?" she gently asks.

"Amazing. Soul was so lovely. We spent every minute together. It was peaceful. I could have lived the rest of my life on that beach."

"I'm sorry. I didn't trust you to make the right choice."

"Thank you."

We share a long hug.

"What are you going to do now?"

"Marry Joa."

"Psalm, you don't have to marry him. We can find you someone else."

"If it isn't Soul, it doesn't matter. Plus, Mom will get what she wants and we can pretend like none of this happened."

"You misjudge her," Novali interjects.

"When you become a mother yourself, you'll understand the nearly animalistic need to protect your children. Things differ from the way she and Dad grew up. We have a lot of freedom. That can be a disadvantage sometimes. She just wants to ensure we are secure as women before she moves on to the next life. You have to at least give her that."

"At some point, she has to trust us to protect ourselves."

"Well, Soul's reputation doesn't do him any favors."

"What happened to not judging a book by its cover?"

"Ha, that's a stupid saying white people made up. Why do books have covers if we're not supposed to consider them?"

Dad hasn't said a word to me since I came home. He is still mad at me. Jazz is not happy with me either, but they will either come around or not. Mom and I can't even be in the same room with each other, so I book a flight and pack my bags. I was supposed to be home days ago myself. Novali is gearing up to leave when she stops by my room.

"The next time we see each other will be at your engagement party."

"I know."

"You don't have to do this."

"Chyna should hear you say that." I laugh.

"Joking isn't going to get you out of this one," Chyna declares, walking into the room.

"What is this an intervention?"

"Yes, Psalm. Don't marry Joa if you know you won't love him," Chyna stresses.

"I promise I'll be a good wife to him."

"That's not what we're worried about," Novali adds.

"There is no love for me, ladies, so I feel like it's better than nothing."

A horn honks outside. "You're going to miss your flight, go."

Novali kisses my cheek and takes the boys out. We watch them go.

Jazz comes to get my bags while Chyna hugs me goodbye. He is stoic when I walk down the stairs.

"Are you going to ignore me the entire drive to the airport?"

"Maybe," he grunts, slamming the trunk and getting into the car.

"Jazz."

"You didn't have to talk to Mom like that."

"Please, you wouldn't last a day in my shoes."

"What's that supposed to mean?"

"Golden boy Jazz won't get what it's like to *always* be at odds with Mom. As a man you get choices I will never have."

"You're right. I don't know what it's like to be a woman or mom's daughter, but that doesn't mean you had to take it that far. Are you really going to keep Mom out of your life?"

"I don't know."

"Don't be so hard," he presses.

"I don't have room to be soft."

"You're a woman."

"Under mom's thumb. She hasn't treated us the same and you know that! Give me some grace."

"I'm sorry Psalm. I just wish there wasn't so much tension between everyone."

He kisses my knuckles in apology, and we spend the rest of the ride in silence. Jazz helps me get my luggage checked before leaving me to find my gate.

I have a long flight to think about what's next. Soul isn't coming back to me and that's my reality, so it's time to make the best of what I have. Mom texts me our dating schedule while I push my bag into the overhead space.

"Here, let me help you."

"Dad! What are you doing here?"

"We need to have a conversation. It'll take longer than the time you had left in LA."

I must be in big trouble if Dad is coming back to Bali with me. It will be nice for us to spend one-on-one time together. Dad had missed his last trip, so it had been nearly a year since he had been in Indonesia. We had a long flight, and he didn't speak a word throughout it. He makes sure to grab anything I need. Dad makes sure to tuck me in and wake me up when we land.

Nothing is on my mind but my greenhouses as we drive back to the compound. The sun is shining, and the air is dewy. My heart feels a little better. The compound gates welcome us, and I take in the expansive land as we drive down the paved roads. The mountains and Lake Bratan are in the distance. This is home. The small truck drives past the vegetation-crowded green and glass houses. The closer we get to my home, the more we drive into the forest. We ride past the towering banyan trees and personal greenhouses to my white and wood mansion.

"When did you move out of the main house?" Dad asks.

"Two years ago, it felt like it was time."

"I know your grandmother isn't happy with that."

"No, she dog-walked me for a long time. I just needed space to grow."

My staff greets me in Indonesian. Dad looks surprised.

"They don't speak Hebrew?"

"No."

He takes tea and sits on the couch, still looking perplexed.

"Living outside of the community, speaking Indonesian in your home. It seems like I don't know you anymore, princess."

"I'm still the same."

"No, you aren't," he softly argues.

"I came here because I want to see why you would want to run away with Soul in the first place. Is there something I could have done to influence your choice?"

Dad let weight take his shoulders, and he wouldn't look at me.

"We were so *worried* when you weren't in your bed that morning. We thought something had happened to you. None of your siblings knew anything. Psalm, I thought I lost you."

"Dad, I was coming back."

"Not good enough. You are angry with your mother because she chose for you but look at what you did when you had the chance to make your own choices."

"One time. Every other choice I've made since the day I was born is with you and Mom's approval. I asked her to let me marry Soul, and she said no. She doesn't get to tell me what to do with my life, and you never stepped in to help me."

"Because she spoke for both of us. We know a lot about that family and knew he would not be good for you. They are too free spirited. I agreed with your mother about it being time for you to settle down, but I trusted you to choose someone good for you."

"I did."

"Oh, princess, you chose with just your heart, and that's where you went wrong."

"Let's forget about all of that now. In time, you will see how great Joa is for you. Now, go relax. The Idrissi family will be visiting soon, and you want to be at your best for them."

My best for them?

That's who my best is for, everybody else. Dad doesn't see me either. That breaks my heart more than my fights with my mom. Dad always gets me. When did he stop?

Since he is staying in the main house, I have the whole house to myself. Rebelliously, I slip into an olive bandeau swimsuit, and my curls cascade down my shoulders. Oh, it feels so good to be home and back in my comfort zone. The towering trees around me feel like a barrier against the outside world. Now I have to pretend like Soul hadn't changed my life. Pretending isn't hard for me. Well, it used to be easy. Since Soul came into my life, it has become harder to pretend. This situation made it clear that when my parents saw the real me, they didn't like what they saw.

My feet swirl around in the cold water, and the calm ultimately returns as soon as I spark up.

Mom has plans for me to spend every appropriate minute with Joa, and Dad is here to be my chaperone. Maybe this is for the best. Maybe Soul and I were just in each other's lives to show each other that love is real and possible. He will eternally be my greatest love, but breaking my own heart every single day by holding on to that love is going to cripple me. Soul has let me go so I can live a life with every perk included. Now that I am back home, it doesn't seem likely that I could give this up. It seems like we were living a fool's dream together. It's time for me to get back to reality, to get back to pretending.

Joa looks so nice in his powder blue tunic, sipping tea in a cafe in Tirta Gangga. He looks like he belongs in this environment.

"You belong in this environment, too," Dad adds, reading my mind.

"It doesn't feel like it."

"That's up to you, princess."

He shakes hands with Joa's father, and Joa pulls out my chair for me.

"It seems like you need some Hibiscus today," he says, sliding the dainty glass across to me.

The tea has the perfect amount of sweetness.

"Psalm, I am going to cut to the chase. Do you honestly want to get married? Or are you still chasing... other things?"

So he knew? Mom's cover job wasn't good enough.

"The only thing I am chasing is VP of Botanical Security and motherhood."

"Are you sure? I'm not going to be played, but we are young. We all make mistakes. It is hard to live by Yah's laws all the time. As long as you are willing to commit to me and our future together, I can forgive the past, and we can move forward."

The future? Quiet nights in the forests of Bali, long walks on the beach, sweet evenings together. Could I forget about Soul? Should I?

Twelve

Soul

MY THINKING TIME is spent thinking about Psalm. Etching everything about her in my mind makes everything we went through feel real. Sometimes, I think she's part of a dream. Dad thought the drive back would clear my head, but I returned with it still in the clouds. By the time I get back, the house is silent. It has never been silent in all of my years. Isra should be back with her husband's family by now, so at least I can avoid her, or so I thought.

"Oh, Soul, you're back," she utters with relief.

For a moment, I am Little Soul again, and Isra is holding me after I scraped my knee.

"I thought you'd be mad at me."

"Of course not. You did what was on your heart. I'm sorry it didn't work out."

"Me too. I miss Psalm so much, Isra."

"I know," she answers.

"The good news is you can move on from this. Go back to New York and clear your head."

"Is it silly I don't want to leave here? All our memories are in LA."

"That's the main reason you should go back. You need to clean your spirit and start a new chapter for yourself. You proved to yourself that you can be a man. No matter what anybody says, you did what men are supposed to do. You just went about it the wrong way this time."

"How do I move on from her?"

"Don't focus on that. Keep your attention on your fourth show and return to your routine. Over time, you will be okay."

Isra helps me book my flight for tomorrow and pack my bags. Mom won't speak a word to me for a while. She is convinced I ruined her reputation with my actions, and maybe I did, but she will come around in time. She normally does. Dad is my first concern, and he is in his office when I interrupt him.

"Soul, how was the drive back?"

"It was therapeutic. I'm going back to New York tomorrow."

"You finally got rid of your creative block."

"I think so."

He slides me a glass of whiskey.

"After this show, we should start my training."

"Are you sure? There is still a lot of time for a lot of shows. Don't pressure yourself."

"It's fine, Dad. Like you say, I can still do art in LA."

"Psalm's not here. She went back to Bali already."

"This isn't about her. It's about me now. I need a new coding computer."

Dad sent me home with some information for me to start working on. It's comforting to see the sketches, data, and semantics. Watching the code trail down the screen reminds me of how much I used to love it. It makes me think of the excitement in Psalm's voice when she talked about her research. The thought of her makes sadness catch in my throat. She would be happy that I am taking things seriously. Psalm reminds me of all the things I love about myself, which includes my work in tech.

Lucky for me, all of my friends are still in town. We usually meet up one more time before we all go our separate ways for a while, but my impromptu trip to Mexico had put a pin in that.

"Well, well, well. If it isn't the runaway bride." Xaevi laughs.

"Fuck off," I drawl.

"Lay off, Xaevi. We're just glad you're back. I can't believe you did it."

"Well, love makes you do crazy things," Kenji adds.

"You have to tell us how it went," Juke presses.

"We went to Mexico and lived in a dream. Psalm is everything I ever wanted, and every day without her is harder than the last."

"You deserve her," Tree adds, and Diana swaps his arm.

"No, Diana. I'm going to say it. Soul, you deserve to fall in love with Psalm. You guys deserve to live happily ever after, and I'm sorry you won't get a chance to."

"Thank you," I whisper, biting back my tears.

"Psalm proved to me that love is possible, and that is enough. For now, I'm going back to New York tomorrow. Then next year, when I return for Kwanzaa, I will stay."

They all look at me with surprise.

"Stay… in LA?"

"It's time for me to come home. There are a lot of places I can take this company. I'm even going back to school for my master's once I settle in."

"We're happy for you," Diana comments.

Were they really? It had to be a sudden change for them.

"So, I'm going to ask what everybody is thinking. Did you smash?" Tree asks.

I threw a beer cap at him.

"No, I would never do such a thing. Psalm's virtue was more important to me than anything. No one will be able to question that."

"They still will, but it looks like it doesn't matter to Joa."

She slides her phone across the table, and there is a picture of their dads, a very subtle way of telling the world that the deal has been sealed.

"Good for them," I reply.

"Soul, it looks like we can fly back together. I have a few meetings in New York," Kenji adds.

The subject is gratefully changed, and we spend the rest of the night enjoying each other's company. All the drama doesn't matter, and I have my last glass of whiskey for the holidays. Tree drops my drunk ass off at home, and Tade is there to help me up the stairs.

"Soul, I'm going to miss you," Tade says when he tosses me on the bed.

"I'll be back, brother, and I'll miss you, too."

He tosses a pillow at me and leaves me to drift off to sleep.

Early the next morning, I board my plane back home and sleep through the entire flight. My manager is angrily waiting for me at the airport.

"If it isn't my favorite MIA client."

"Hello, Walter."

"Soul, where the hell have you been?"

"Dealing with family things and life. Don't ask me too many questions."

"Can I ask you how far along you are in your theme? We need to start booking venues, caterers..."

"Walter, I literally stepped off the plane ten seconds ago."

"Yeah, and you are already behind. This hasn't happened before. Normally, we are knee-deep in planning. Right now, half the projects would be planned."

"Well, every artist has a dark streak. Take me home."

Walter angrily sighs but drops me off at my apartment in Manhattan. The concierge greets me as I take the elevator to the top floor. This apartment had been my crowning achievement before. It's proof that I made it outside of the Nation. It's a disrespect to everything we had sacrificed to build ourselves to where we are now. It isn't just the work of the royal family that makes us a global conglomerate. It's every last one of us. It was wrong for me to fight away from it all. Everything about me is from them. Still, the apartment fits my 70s pimp aesthetic with the copper and colored-toned walls, orange-toned carpet and classic brown furniture. The 360 city views remind me that I am on top of the world and it's so lonely without Psalm.

Silence stretches throughout the three-bedroom apartment, and it's too much for me to bear, so I go to my studio in Brooklyn. The streets are packed. People are laughing and spilling out of bars or walking down the streets holding hands.

The city is alive, which typically fuels me, but now we feel disconnected. The insignificant brown brick building has been my home away from home. My studio is separated into rooms — one for painting or sculpting, another for drawing, and one for finishing. Of course, there are rooms for relaxing, eating, and storage. I spent so much time here that we had to install a shower last year. The graffiti-littered walls greet me, shutting the cold air outside. I need to get Psalm out of my head. I need to find a place for my love to go, so I start with modeling. It feels good to have the clay back in my hands.

Her face comes to me easily in rough forms first. Then, the arch of her brow and the curve of her lips through the fine-tuning. Those eyes tell me everything when she is surprised when she is happy or sad. They are the window to her soul, so it's only right I do them justice. Psalm is a mosaic of a woman, and it would be hard to represent her in one project, so she will be the theme of my fourth show, and none of the pieces will be for sale. No one will know the theme but me. This will be my therapy and my final goodbye to the woman who owns my heart.

Thirteen

Psalm

ONE YEAR Later

It's time for Kwanzaa again, and this time, I am an engaged woman. Last year isn't on my mind. It its a new year, and things have gotten better. My fingers refreshed my email for the thousandth time today. The position of vice president of BS is open and available. No one is more qualified than me. Only three of us are up for the position, but my research should give me an edge. Besides work, courting has been my main focus. Joa and I have been living a wonderful life together so far. His mother is our constant shadow, but today, she allows us to have a moment alone.

"Psalm, are you all packed? We have to go," Joa asks.

"I'm almost ready."

"Funny, I don't see any bags."

"I'm sorry. I am supposed to hear back about my application soon, and I wanted to check in a few more times. "

"You're a shoo-in. Now, come on. We have to catch our flight soon."

Joa leaves me to finish packing, and I smile sadly at his retreating frame. We have taken things slowly and grew fond of each other, but this isn't love. My heart was hoping that Joa's charm would wipe away all the things I had for Soul, but he is still there whenever I have a taco, get out in the waves, or listen to Stevie Wonder his face is there. It brings me to tears sometimes. I want to move on, but my heart won't let me. I am being haunted at this point.

My life is good. Our research has taken us very far and got noticed by the royal family. This is my chance to accomplish my dream. Joa has made equal leaps in his career. Our time together is therapeutic. He is a kind and patient man. We have fun together, but life with him is mundane. It's average. It is nights with quiet dinners, shared reading, and sunsets by the pool. It is an enjoyable life, but it isn't the one I am sure I want.

Also, if I get this position, I will have to move to LA officially for eight months out of the year. My job will get a lot more strenuous and there will be less time for us to spend together, so it will be like the life I usually live with the occasional visit from my companion. That isn't a marriage. That isn't happiness, but I don't know what else to do. Joa is happy with who I am now. My parents are happy with this Psalm. My community will be happy with this union, so why isn't my heart in it?

We make it to the airport just in time and board the Nation plane before takeoff. Sleep takes me almost as soon as my butt hits the seat.

A soft hand jolts me awake.

"How long was I out?"

"Nearly the entire flight. We're landing soon." Joa chuckles before heading to the bathroom.

We are going to spend the day with our families before the engagement party tomorrow. Novali is already home and waiting for me. Joa clears his throat before speaking on the drive to my home.

"Our party tomorrow is going to make everything official. Are you ready for that?"

"Of course, we've been planning it for a year now. It's about time."

"I'm excited to spend the rest of my life with you," he adds.

"And I you."

Joa kisses my cheek before dropping me off at the door. Mom and I haven't spoken all year, outside of marriage stuff. It isn't that I am still mad. I just don't have the energy to repair our relationship right now.

Novali turns around as soon as she hears the door close.

"Psalm, you're home!"

"And you're pregnant!" I exclaim, rubbing her round belly.

"I wanted to surprise you."

"*We* wanted to surprise you," Chyna says, coming around the corner with her own round belly.

We jump up and down, screaming in delight together.

"It sounds like someone is killing penguins in here," Jazz exclaims, coming out of the kitchen.

He pulls me into a tight hug.

"So much to celebrate," Mom says, interrupting our squealing.

Everyone leaves us to talk.

"Tomorrow, we announce your engagement to the entire community. There will be no going back then."

"I know."

We sit in awkward silence for a moment.

"I know you think I don't love you, Psalm, but I love you more than you'll ever know." She closed the distance between us.

"You have consistently been my stubborn child. It's the reason we bump heads so often. No matter what happens between us I will never stop loving you. Everything I do for you is because I want to protect your spirit. You love like no other. You are brave, bold, and beautiful. The wrong man can rob you of that. It's my job to ensure that doesn't happen, so even if you never speak to me again, I will know I did my job."

"You should have let me help you. Now, I don't know if we will ever be the same."

"In time, we can be. Trust me on that," she answers with a smile.

Soul

"I can't believe we are packing this place up," Walter says.

"Well, I am a man of my word."

The Brooklyn Studio had been packed up. It was going to be sold soon.

"You still don't want to tell me your theme?"

"Nope."

He chuckles and shakes his head. "Whatever it is, this is your best one yet."

"I agree."

Walter's belly laughs.

"I never thought I would see the day you agreed with me."

"I am a changed man."

"We will see about that," he says, leaving me to do the final walk-through.

Fourteen pieces. All of them covering a piece of her personality. This will be the first show my family comes to. It's also my first show in LA. We have purchased a studio in LA. Walter bought me a home as well. Of course, I will be returning to my in-house suite, but having my own space is crucial to my sanity. Selling my apartment in Manhattan is the biggest pang. It is the final nail in my New York coffin and the end of my chapter of running. Dad and I got me up to speed on all of the company's systems. My onboarding is nearly complete. It's time for the old man to retire.

Walter blessed me by moving to LA permanently for my art. All of my fans think the move is classic Soul. They are excited to see what this change of venue will bring, and so am I. There is only one disappointment that stays with me. I still love her. No matter how many pieces I create, the love doesn't go away. I feel haunted by my broken heart. It's probably time for some real therapy.

Psalm is getting married for sure now. I had heard whispers of her engagement party. Once they come out to the entire community, that's it. There will be no running without staining the family name. I have one more day until she will be out of my reach forever. The pang in my heart doesn't hurt as much as when she left me in Mexico, but it still hurts. Hopefully, once the show closes, so will my love for her.

My show is opening tonight, so there is a lot to do. We have to put it all together before I meet with Tree to celebrate. Everyone won't be in town until tomorrow. The show will be open for three weeks, hosted by the Los Angeles Art Museum. It's a big move for my art career. Being a professional artist was nice, but I will have to scale it back now that I am onboarding in person. It's time to become my full self, including making time for all of me. I will be back in my family's daily lives, away from all the things that kept me distracted, and back with my friends. Everything is falling into place.

My team is hard at work when I walk into the expansive room.

"Soul, thank God you are here. We are having issues with the lighting."

Walter and I supervise the delivery of the pieces, work on the perfect lighting, and put everything into place. It's brilliant. The walk through the room takes you through our relationship. Each guest will stroll past all the stages she drifted through as our relationship progressed, down to the time we said goodbye.

"Whoever this woman is, you must really miss her," Walter says.

"Every day. This is supposed to be my goodbye."

"It feels more like an homage."

"That works, too."

My eyes catch the marble that holds her exact likeness. It had taken me an entire year to finish this sculpture. It's the last piece I completed. It's the way Psalm wants the world to see her, the one she thinks people love the most, but she's wrong. It is only a corner of the picture. Her full picture is more than that.

"You can't be in there!" We hear security shout.

A pregnant woman rounds the corner.

"Fuck off!" she growls, shaking off the security guard.

"Chyna?" I exclaim.

"Soul, long time no see. Growing out the sides is a good idea," she says, motioning to my hair.

"What are you doing here?"

"You know Psalm's engagement party is tomorrow?"

"No, I didn't know, but what's it to me?"

"Don't you still love her?"

I opened my mouth to answer but noticed all the stares in the room.

"Get out," I say.

Walter rushes everyone out of the room. Chyna looks around. No doubt she will know that every piece is about Psalm.

"Of course, I still love her, but we already went our separate ways, Chyna. There is nothing I can do."

"She still loves you, too. In fact, she is marrying Joa in hopes that her feelings will go away, but it has been a year already. You have not left her heart."

"What do you want me to do?"

"I want you to save everyone. Save you and Psalm from a lifetime without each other. Save Joa from a life with a woman who can't love him and save my mother from a life without one of her daughters. Be the hero," she states before walking away.

If only being the hero were that easy.

———————

"Soul, you got this. The preview show in New York went great. Everyone is excited to see what you have been working on. Don't overthink it now." Walter says.

"This is the first time my whole family will see my work."

"They are going to love it. Just... enjoy tonight. You routinely get too stressed before shows."

Walter goes to open the doors, and my heart is beating outside of my chest. To everyone else, this theme is a celebration of the Black woman and commentary on the opinions swirling around her, but for all the people who knew, this is my love letter to Psalm Rose. Too bad she will not be here to see it.

I hear the people before I see them. It is a symphony of gasps and awed whispers. It's music to my ears each time. The wait staff immediately went around with drinks and appetizers. I have seen curators, art reviewers, and regular buyers, everyone but the people who matter the most. Finally, Isra comes into view. She is the first person to find me.

"You really love her, huh?"

"Could you tell?" I joke.

We share a laugh.

"Really, Soul, you truly see her for who she is. That's a hard thing to do."

"Not when you love someone."

She pats my arm in agreement and goes to see the rest of the exhibit.

"Soul!" my dad calls out. "This is brilliant. I can't wait to see the rest. You outdid yourself this time."

"This time?" I comment, puzzled.

"You think I would ever miss one of your shows?"

"This isn't your first one?"

"No, son. I've been to all of your shows. Who do you think brought all of your first pieces?"

"That was you?"

He laughs at my expression. There was a mystery donor from every show who paid over the asking price for my first piece. I just thought it was some eccentric millionaire, but of course, it's my dad.

"I told you I am perpetually proud of you, and I mean that," he expresses.

We share a hug before he goes to finish the exhibit. My eyes are searching for my mother next. She has barely spoken to me this year, but there she is, standing by the oil painting.

"Do you like it?"

"It's certainly different from anything your father has brought home before."

"Mom, I'm sorry for last year. I just wanted to be my own man."

"You've always been yours. Even as a baby, you would cry if we tried to hold you sometimes. I expected you to rebel, just not like that."

"Can you forgive me?"

"Well, you're moving back home, taking over for your father, so I guess you are forgiven." I pull her into my arms as she chuckles. "Come, take me to see the rest. She really is a perfect muse."

Psalm

"Novali, I don't want to go out tonight. It's not like we can party with you in this condition."

"It's not a *party* party. It's a small jazz show. They opened a new cigar bar in downtown LA. This is the only night there will be no smoking."

"Why can't Kocoum go with you?"

"Well, I wanted to save this for the dinner table, but he got transferred, and we're moving back to the States!"

I drop my lip gloss and scream.

"Don't tell anyone, but he's packing up our life in Paris."

"That means we will be together again if I get this job."

"Yes, yes, all the more reason for us to celebrate."

"Alright, I'll go."

Novali squeals before running off to get dressed.

Tonight is my last night as a free woman, so I feel like this is the perfect night to wear his gift. After this, it will go into storage, a moment for me to relive from time to time. I should be happy. Tomorrow, both of our families will bless our potential union. Four months after that, we'll get married. This engagement has been long enough for both families, and it's time for us to wrap this up with a marriage. That almost makes me hyperventilate. I need to stand by this choice. If I don't marry Joa, I will spend the rest of my life comparing every man to Soul. It will be impossible for me to get married. My mom will hate that, for sure.

The gold highlights strewn throughout the abaya accentuate the blood-orange material. Each layer sits on my skin like a cloud, and my burgundy makeup compliments it perfectly. This is how Soul saw me — elegant, regal, whole. I want to hold on to the time I got to be a complete person. A time when I was more than what people wanted me to be. Tonight, I will have fun with my sister and mourn that Psalm I got to be. Tonight is her last night alive.

"You look perfect," Novali compliments, adjusting my head wrap.

"Let's go. We don't want to be late."

Novali talks a mile a minute about being back home, bonding with Chyna over babies, and the boys' accomplishments. It's a pleasant distraction from my swirling thoughts. While she is talking I notice we arrive at the art museum.

"I thought we were going to the cigar bar."

"Since it's a non-smoking night, they are hosting it here."

That's odd, but whatever. Novali was odd during the last pregnancy, too.

Once we walk in the door, I know she's a liar. This is not the cigar bar. This is Soul's latest show.

"You lied to me." I chuckle.

"I wanted you to see that he hadn't forgotten about you."

"Novali..."

"Just hear me out. I was on Mom's side because Soul's reputation worried me, but I kept tabs on him. He's moved back home and is taking over the business. He's responsible, and he loves you. Mom can make this sacrifice, but you can't."

"This is not just about mom."

"Exactly. This is about all of us. The Nation was founded to give all of us a chance at a better life. What chance is it if you don't get to choose? I married Kocoum because I knew we could love each other. Jazz married Sherie for the same reason. You found someone who is good, and you should be able to have him."

"Novali, Soul left me. He doesn't want me."

"Take a walk through this exhibit, then tell me that's true."

She turns me around to face a sculpture of me, without a doubt. There are my eyes, lips, and nose, along with my thoughtful expression. The abaya draping the statue is starkly traditional and gold. It was the first night he saw me. It is when I introduced him to the Psalm everybody gets. It brings tears to my eyes because even under all that tradition my true self shines through in my ear piercings and smirk. At every turn, there is some part of me. A painting caught my eye. It's called "A Secular Woman."

My hair is splayed across the canvas with a hint of a blue sky above and an ocean below. Soul had used texture with the paint to create my curls perfectly. Hair is the most intimate part of womanhood. Yah had blessed us with our crowning glory. Only a few got to see it uncovered, so it is quite secular indeed that Soul has seen it. To the left of me is a chair with a black wooden doll and a lone blue guitar next to it.

Soul had painted a lone pair of white headphones in bright pastel colors. It is stark on the white canvas. That day had been colorful. My love for greenery is displayed in the ropes of braided vines dangling from the ceiling. None of this could be put into words. All of what we felt had to be translated into art like this. It seems criminal to give up on a love like this one. I walked through pale sand strewn with blacked out polaroids and empty vials. It was a nod to the mementos we made. The last piece is a clear jar filled with black paint. There is no nameplate for it.

There was no name for the pain that I felt in those early days. It's like being in a sensory deprivation chamber or being in a void. That jar represents all the things I have felt since he walked away from me. Suddenly, I feel eyes on me. Soul is standing not too far away. He is growing his hair out but looks completely the same when he gazes at me. He is still in love.

Isolation is the best part of this day.

The morning is for me. It makes me think of my woman's day bath. I felt like a different woman back then. Now, I have known love and adoration. All the anger has boiled out of me. I'm not mad at my mom anymore and don't want to spend my days hiding in Bali. I feel more whole today than I have in a long time. Soul's love for me will keep me company on my lonely days with Joa. His laugh will remind me to smile when I am sad and to enjoy the things that make me happy.

My head slips under the warm bath water, and I hold my breath. *This is it. This is it.* Today, there would be no looking back. After today, we will forever dream about what we could have been. As long as I am taking Soul's love with me, then it doesn't matter. We will meet in each other's dreams. Maybe in the afterlife, we can be with each other again.

My phone dings, causing me to come up for air. The dry towel clears my vision. It's an email from the botanical department. My fingers shake as I open it.

"Dear Miss Rose, we are excited to invite you to the team as Vice President of Botanical Security. We understand that our young people are the future, and based on your experience and dedication, you are the perfect person for the job," I read out loud.

It is a dream come true after years of putting my nose to the ground. I missed parties, family milestones, and time to myself, and made countless other sacrifices for this moment. There were three people up for the position, and they selected me. The first person I want to tell is Soul. He had been so excited about my research, and he'd have been so proud of me. He would've shouted to the heavens. He would've thanked Yah for blessing me with my talent. He would've danced to my success.

I caught the tear before it got too far away from me. This will not be a day to think about Soul. Joa at least deserves my full attention today. I will not let this be a loss for him. I will be a model wife and partner for him in this marriage. I will celebrate his wins, push him to chase his dreams, and bear his children, but I am sure now I will never be in love with him. I think deep down, he knows that. Joa loves me. He had admitted it to me before but would not let me comment on it after which is all the proof I need. He wanted to believe the illusion so we would play pretend together for the rest of our lives.

"Psalm, move your ass," Chyna exclaims, holding out a towel to me.

"We have time."

"Time is an illusion, and your makeup is going to take forever."

Novali, Chyna, and Mom are in charge of the lavish makeup process. Mom had draped the entire room in silks and satins. A small mirror is surrounded by the makeup bowls. They covered the floor with plush pillows. Chyna drapes a robe around my shoulders before sitting me in the middle. We sit in silence as they work. Mom does my hair, and Novali starts on my makeup, discreetly wiping my tears away as she works.

"Psalm, are you... sure you want to go through with this? You don't have to prove anything to me."

"This isn't about you, Mom."

"I know, I just mean... you should be happy."

"I am, really. Don't worry about me."

She doesn't ask me again, but it warms my heart that she did ask. It sounded genuine. There is hope for us to find forgiveness with each other yet.

"Thank you for being a great mom to me, and I'm sorry for being a brat."

"All is forgiven, baby girl. I'm sorry too. I should have trusted you more."

"If you ruin my masterpiece, I am going to murder you," Novali threatens dabbing at another tear.

That causes us to burst out in laughter. Chyna turns up the music, and they get back to work. Mom dips every other finger in henna. Novali finished my braids and adorned each one with jewels and copper hair jewelry. The silk seafoam green abaya is fitted at the waist with a dramatic ball gown skirt. The bodice drifts into delicate tulle and silk pink flowers. Petals and the nude silk gave the illusion of a bouquet silhouette. Mom clips the loose head wrap around my braids. Once we are officially engaged, the head wrap will come off.

"You look breathtaking," Mom whispers around her tears.

"He will be lucky to have you," Chyna adds.

We dab each other's tears.

"Go into prayer. We are going to get dressed."

Mom pushes me into the prayer room, and I thank Yah for all the love I have in my life and for the peace to come. I am so grateful. Joa could have cast me aside. His family could have exposed me. Soul could have exposed me, but I am blessed enough to have their forgiveness and protection. Some women have done less than me and ended up in worse situations. Dad comes to get me out of the prayer closet, and he catches his breath.

"You look astonishing, princess."

Dad dips the paintbrush into a bottle, painting a white line down my face, through my lips, and ending at my chin.

"You're going to do great," he whispers.

Dad walks me down the stairs to the waiting family, spouses included.

"Psalm..." Sherie breaths

"Wow!" Abraham gasps.

Jazz wipes away his tears as he helps me down the rest of the stairs into my high heels.

"To the venue, we go," Chyna grumbles. She wants a happy ending, but one day, she will see I got one.

We don't speak during the drive-over Mom surprises us by pulling a flask from her purse and offering it to me.

"It'll help with the jitters."

She must have seen my hands shaking. I am still trembling when Jazz helps me out of the car. We have time to put the finishing touches on our looks and do the final blessing ceremonies. With an hour left until the end of my time, Mom deep breathes me into the room and starts the last ritual before Joa and I will be bound together forever.

Soul

Two hours and she will be gone. I am sitting outside around where we had our bonfire last year. Chyna told me the exact time it starts, and I find myself counting down the minutes.

"Soul, what are you doing here?" Tree shouts.

"I was relaxing until you started yelling."

"You have two hours to get to the venue, and I know that's not what you're going to wear."

"Tree, I am not going to stop their engagement."

"So you are going to let some man spend the rest of his life married to the woman you love?"

"It's what Psalm wants."

"She wants you! We both saw the look on her face at the exhibit. She still loves you, and that's worth fighting for."

"We did all of our fighting. Let me mourn."

"When you're an old dusty ass man, you're going to wish you did all you could. Soul, you are not meant for a mediocre life or love. Go after what you want."

Tree waits for a moment and storms off at my inaction. He would understand later. They all would.

"You know, he has a point," Dad states behind me.

"What? Last year, you were telling me to forget her."

"I've watched you grow over the last year into your whole self. This is the Soul that's ready for marriage. I saw glimpses of him last year. I should have had your back then. I'm sorry, and I have your back now. Get changed."

With my dad's blessing, I took the stairs two at a time. Someone else is willing to fight with us. That development spurred me on. I don't want to spend the rest of my life wishing I had fought for her until the last second. I tried to forget. I poured all my love for her into my art, hoping it would cure me, but it has only made me sicker. I chose cream-colored slacks and a seafoam green tunic as my fit. Dad was waiting for me at the bottom of the stairs.

"You look great. You look like a man." He sighs with pride before we sprint out to the car. We are down to an hour.

"She isn't the only one you have to convince in there. Make sure her family feels secure, too. If you really want this, you need to convince all of them," he advises.

Another valid point. I had wronged the entire family by putting blind love first. This time, I will do things the right way.

It seems like everyone in LA decided to take the streets at the same time. When we were about a block from the venue, traffic completely stalls.

"You'll have to walk from here, or you'll never make it. Good luck," Dad says.

I tore out of the car and sprinted down the street. I don't care if I look out of my mind or if someone from the community sees me. This is my last chance to tell Psalm I love her, and I won't miss this for anything.

The building comes into view, and relief spreads through my chest. I know it's going to be heavily guarded, but I have to find a way inside. I run right past Chyna, and she calls after me.

"For the love of Yah, I thought you were dumb enough not to come," she chastises.

"We're almost out of time," I choke out.

She pulls me into the building, guiding me around friends and family from either side. My vision is blurring, and adrenaline is rushing through my body. This is my last stand.

"Chyna, what are you doing?"

"There is no time. Jazz let us through."

"No way this is the jackass that took Psalm to Mexico." Jazz growls.

Chyna pushes him back. "We don't have time for this Jazz. They love each other and should get to be together."

"Please, let me say my peace. If you don't like what I have to say, then I'll leave, and no one has to know I'm here."

"Psalm has found happiness with Joa. You are not going to ruin that. Get. Out."

"If you think Psalm is happy, you are a terrible big brother."

That takes the wind out of his sails.

"You get two minutes. No more. No less."

Chyna looks grateful and pushes open the doors. Psalm's gentle scent rushes out to greet me, and we stand face-to-face for the first time in nearly a year.

"Psalm, I can't let you walk away with him without giving this one last shot," I declare, then turn around the room. "It is my deepest regret that I did things the wrong way with Psalm. I let my heart lead me down a path of irrational decisions. I am the most sorry to you, Mrs. Rose. You set out to protect your children, to give them the safest, fullest life. By taking Psalm away, I pretended to know more than you. If you can find it in your heart, please forgive me. There is nothing more important to me than her happiness and safety. If you allow it, I will spend the rest of my life proving to you that you made no mistake in allowing me to have her hand."

I took another step toward Psalm.

"To you, Song Flower, I promise never to leave you again. It was wrong of me to turn away from you. Psalm, I love you. I love everything about you, from your humor to your passion. There is no one on this earth I would rather share my life with than you. I want every part of life with you, and if you'll have me I'll spend every day showing you why I am the best choice."

She is crying, her makeup lightly streaked.

"Oh, Soul, it's too late."

"It doesn't have to be. We still have ten minutes."

A laugh breaks up her tears.

"Trust me," I beg.

Psalm walks up to her father. "Please, Daddy, I will never ask you for anything else. Please let me have this one."

"Mr. Rose, I will spend the rest of my life proving to you that your daughter is safe with me."

Her mom surprises me by approaching her husband as well. "Let her."

"Are you sure this is what you want, princess?"

"More than anything in the world."

Psalm turns to me. "I spent the entire year trying to forget Soul. I don't want to hurt anymore. I want to be happy. Let me be happy."

"What about your family, Soul? Will they approve?" her mom asks.

"We approve and will be more than happy to join our families," my dad states, putting his hand on my shoulder.

"Alright, you have my blessing," her dad whispers.

Psalm sprints into my arms, her tears in full flow. As soon as her body touches mine, I feel whole. I feel real. She kisses me passionately, causing her sisters to squeal, but we don't hear them. We are too busy drifting into forever.

The End